SAM HAWKINS
PIRATE DETECTIVE

*The Case of the
Cut Glass Cutlass*

By Ian Billings
Illustrated by Chris White

CABOODLE BOOKS LTD

First published in 2003 by Macmillan Children's Books
This edition published in Great Britain in 2009
by Caboodle Books Ltd

A Catalogue record for this book is available from the
British Library.

ISBN-13: 978-0-9562656-7-8

Typeset in Century by Paul Wilson

Printed in the UK by CPI Cox & Wyman, Reading

The paper and board used in the paperback by Caboodle Books Ltd
are natural recyclable products made from wood grown in sustain-
able forests. The manufacturing processes conform to the environ-
mental regulations of the country of origin.

Caboodle Books Ltd
Riversdale, 8 Rivock Avenue,
Steeton, BD20 6SA, U.K.
Tel: +44 (0) 1535 656015

www.authorsabroad.com

Ian Billings was born at a very young age. He has done many things in his time and some of them he'd like to tell you about. He is an ex-juggler, a pantomime writer (fifty productions!), an actor, TV extra, a theatre technician, a university lecturer, a model and a general dabbler in many areas.

He has written episodes of BBC TV's Chuckle-Vision and his stage plays and pantomimes have been performed in Wolverhampton, Northampton, Hastings, Nottingham, Weston-Super-Mare and on a ferry to Spain. He has a Masters Degree from Birmingham University and two goldfish from Petworld. He is five feet and seven inches in length and avoids cheese.

In 2007 he began performing stand-up comedy for kids at Edinburgh Festival Fringe (whilst also presenting his own radio show for Festival FM!) and now he tours theatres and schools throughout the UK, Cyprus, Germany and in 2009, Australia. He was described by one young audience member as "the most imaginative adult I've ever met!"

Visit him at www.ianbillings.com

OTHER BOOKS INCLUDE -
SAM HAWKINS, PIRATE DETECTIVE,
AND THE POINTY HEAD LIGHTHOUSE
DON'T DIS MISS
PIRATE STORIES
MERMAID STORIES
BALLERINA STORIES

CHAPTER ONE

Call me Hawkins. Sam Hawkins. The finest swashbuckler ever to sail the seven seas. Once my name struck fear into the hearts of the bravest sailors. Once my life was one of plunder and pillage and passion. But no more.

My family goes back a long way, and each and every one was a pirate. The Hawkinses have spliced and sliced their way through history and many of them have become legends. Great Uncle 'Tweaker' Hawkins – terror of the South Seas – Grandaddy 'Slurper' Hawkins – peril of the North Sea – and, of course, Maiden Aunt 'Knitter' Hawkins, who could moan a man into submission at twenty paces. But the most famous of all was my dear mother, 'Grapeshot' Betty Hawkins, who could throw a coconut 100 yards and burp a baby at the same time. God bless her! I can see her now: four feet six inches in her socks, a thick cigar hanging beneath her moustache and a face like a sack of spuds. I'll never meet her like again.

Generations of Hawkinses had lived a long and naughty life on the distant Caribbean Island of Jataka. But soon after the nasty events of the Custard Powder Party (in which 'Mad Duck' Hawkins upended thirty-nine barrels of the governor's finest illegal custard into the sea) we were deported, lock, stock and thirty-nine empty barrels, back to England – a home we hadn't set eyes on for 200 years. And here I was born. The rest of the Hawkinses soon grew weary of England, some got normal jobs, and many died of a broken heart. But not I. I plundered on – until the day my ship exploded. The good ship Scuttle Butt was blasted from the waters by a loathsome pirate with whose name I won't soil these pages. Pah! So I threw in the anchor and settled for a landlubbing life aboard the Naughty Lass – a fine old council house in Puddle Lane, Washed-upon-the- Beach. Decorated up, it could easily be mistaken for a ship. With all the nautical clutter I'd accumulated from years at sea, my new home was everything an old sea-salt could have wished for.

And that is where my story really begins.

Gloomy storm clouds were looming over the Naughty Lass the day I set sail on the tale I am about to tell. Lan Ho, my Chinese sea cook and cabin boy, was on the roof, his little hand clasping a television aerial which had recently been snapped off by the fierce westerly wind. Good old Ho. As the punishing wind battered his little body he clung bravely to the aerial and to his task.

I, being the captain and leader of my team, sat snugly in the hold with a mug of foaming grog in my hand. Before me was the televisual entertainment box. TV as you call it. All I could see on the screen was a snowy blizzard worse than any arctic winter.

From outside I heard Lan Ho's straining voice.

'Is that better?'

'No,' I said, sipping my grog. 'Try a-pointing nor'- nor'-west!'

'Which way is that?' came the reply.

'Towards the cliffs!'

Lan Ho was clinging on up there, muttering Chinese oaths under his breath.

'Is that better?' he yelled.

Before me on the screen a figure shimmered into view. 'Twas a comely wench with beautiful blonde hair. She was playing the trumpet. The picture came clearer and I saw 'twas not a trumpet but one of those micronophones for making words louder. This is what she said.

'. . . in a terrible incident, Washed-upon-the-Beach's museum was broken into last night and its prize exhibit stolen.'

The picture changed to that of a sword, nay, a cutlass.

'. . . The famous Cut-glass Cutlass, once owned by Greenbeard the Pirate and recently bought by the museum.'

I couldn't believe my eyes. I sat bolt upright and stared. This was the Cut-glass Cutlass. The finest and most revered weapon ever held by a buccaneer. It had cut and thrust its way across the seven seas and caused chaos in every corner of the globe. Many ask how such a delicate object could be used for such purposes, but legend tells that the weapon was fashioned from the toughest, most beautiful glass ever made – a strange mixture of glass, diamond, glue and rhino horn. And how do I know this? Because it used to belong to Grapeshot Betty – otherwise known as Betty Hawkins, my mum. She had wrested it from the sock drawer of the great Greenbeard himself. I gazed up at the portrait of her on the mantelpiece.

'Look, Mum,' I said. 'Imagine what that would be worth now!'

'£300,000! £300,000!' shrieked a voice over my starboard shoulder. 'Twas only Spot the Parrot, repeating the words of the television reporter.

The picture changed once more to show a small, balding man dabbing at his eyes with a handkerchief. His shiny, sweaty head made him look like a dolphin emerging from the briny. 'I have with me here Horace Silk, curator of the museum. How are you feeling at this moment, Mr Silk?' asked the interviewer.

The man blew a loud blast into his hanky.

'It was all meant to be a surprise. We'd kept quiet about the purchase of the cutlass, because we wanted it to be the main attraction at the Mayor's show. All the little kiddies could have seen it. And it . . . and it . . . Oh dear, I can't speak.'

The camera returned to the woman.

'So that's the latest from today's big story. Now it's back to the studio.'

But I heard and saw no more. There it was, before my very eyes. My old mother's sword. The number of times she'd lovingly sat me on her knee and we'd sharpened it together!

She'd spit an ounce of tobacco into a nearby knitting basket and draw me close. The cutlass would glint in the moonlight and she'd say, 'One day, Samuel, when I've gone to a watery grave, this will be yours. Mind you treat it well.'

'Yes, Mother,' I'd say, prising the gin bottle from her hand and carefully replacing the cork. I'd help her totter to bed and spend the rest of the evening polishing and caring for the Cutglass Cutlass.

The day my mother was swallowed by a whale is one I shall remember all my life. A splash, a scream and a burp and she was no more. My dear mother had disappeared and so had the cutlass. I had wondered for many a year what had become of it.

'Twas at that precise moment I saw my future. I gazed into the imitation log fire as the flames revolved and pondered my thoughts.

Then the penny dropped. Plop!

It seemed so obvious. I had all the skills, I had all the knowledge. It was the perfect job for a retired seaman. I leaped to my feet and raised my mug in the air.

'I shall become Sam Hawkins, Pirate Detective!'

Some grog slopped on my head.

'Parrot Detective! Parrot Detective!' shrieked Spot.

From outside I heard a straining Chinese voice.

'Can I come down now?'

☠ ☠

I couldn't sleep a wink that night. I tossed and tumbled in my hammock and fell out twice. I was so seized by my new idea that sleep only got in the way. Before long I rose, lit a candle, sat at my aged writing desk, which had been around the world with me, and began to write. I dipped my quill into an inkpot and looked out through the porthole. The storm was crashing and smashing at the glass and I could barely see the lights of the church beyond. The swirling rain joined with my swirling thoughts and I set to my task. As the Naughty Lass slumbered I set to a-writing the plans for my new life. And these were they:

Buy a magnifying glass.

Eat more greens.

Befriend the local police — become hearty and chummy with them and try to extract information on unsolved cases.

Try to be more eagle-eyed.

Buy a raincoat. And a disguise kit. Especially a beard.

Try walking stealthily.

Get some fingerprint dust. Old gunpowder will do.

Always be alert and vigilant.

My writing started to fail here and tiredness consumed me. My mind was a whirlpool of dreams and ideas. Outside, the storm was subsiding and over the horizon the twinkling light of daybreak could be seen. Blissfully happy, I blew out the candle and set sail for the sea of dreams.

My head clunked as it hit the desk.

'Cock-a-doodle-do!'

I woke with a start and tried to remember why I wasn't in my hammock.

'Cock-a-doodle-*doodle*-do!'

Blast that parrot.

'Quiet, Spot!' I muttered blearily. I felt my bristles and a cold draught coming from the window.

I gazed down at my desk. The page became clearer and suddenly all last night's thoughts came tumbling and stumbling back into my mind. I grinned to myself. 'Sam Hawkins, Pirate Detective.' I tasted the words, and wiped a little dribble from my chin.

In the galley Lan Ho was evolving something in his wok. Good old Ho. He was my oriental sidekick and a finer side to kick I've yet to find. He was an endearing fellow – the body of a youngster and the head of a wise man. The poor boy was an orphan and had seen and done more in his short time on earth than many twice his age. In times of crisis Ho's nimble mind and everpresent catapult have proved invaluable. Eleven years ago I'd found him as a baby, floating in a small basket in Kowloon Bay, Hong Kong. Since I saved his life that day he has been endlessly grateful to me.

He stomped into the living room and slapped a plate before me.

'Of all the people I had to be rescued by, it had to be you!' he said.

He likes to joke with me this way.

'Breakfast!' he said, pointing at the brown, bubbling lump on the plate.

'And what, pray tell, is it?'

Lan Ho always tried to please.

'It's breakfast. Duh!' he said, placing his tongue behind his lower lip and pushing it forward in that delightful way he has.

I grabbed a chopstick and poked the lump. I expected it to yelp, leap off the plate and scuttle back to the garden pond. It merely let out a sound like a deflating tyre. I removed something small and brown and examined it.

'Sausage?' I enquired.

'Of course! Best Cumberland sausage. The supermarket was throwing it out so I got it cheap! And there's a cherry! Can you smell the vanilla? That's your favourite.'

I slapped down my chopstick and set my beady gaze on my assistant.

'Vanilla ice cream?'

'Not vanilla ice cream, sir. No, it's vanilla yoghurt. Low fat! I'm going to put you on diet!'

I leaned back in my chair and sighed.

'Sausage, cherries and vanilla yoghurt? And what do you call this strange and bizarre concoction?'

'Breakfast. Duh! Eat it up – it's good for you!'

Suddenly the other door was thrown open and there, framed in the doorway, was Molly Meakins.

'Molly, my dear!'

Now what can I tell you of old Molly? A stout and noble woman. Built like a rum barrel and with a fist that could squeeze mud from a bone. She was renowned throughout the piratical world as the brawniest woman ever to swash a buckle. No pirate worth his salt would tangle with Molly. She was the finest sailor at sea. She could tie a sheepshank with one hand and once dragged a ten -foot whale from Bristol to Southampton, though no one knows why. I first came across Molly on a trawler bound for Norway – she had been dragged out of the sea with two tons of cod. She'd no idea how she'd got there and reeked of whisky. But I rescued her from her fishy fate and she has been devoted to me ever since.

'Where's my breakfast, Hawkins?' Molly growled.

'Lan Ho was just . . .'

'Where's my breakfast, Lan Ho?'

'It's on its way,' explained Ho.

He took away my untouched breakfast, slopped it on to a clean plate and handed it to Molly.

'Breakfast!' he announced.

She swallowed it in three mouthfuls.

I straightened my neckerchief and coughed. Now was the perfect moment to announce my announcement.

'I'm glad we're all here, my merry bunch of cutthroats . . .'

'Yo-ho-ho!' said Lan Ho, raising a mug.

'. . . for I have an important announcement that is to change the course of our life's voyage.'

Lan Ho and Molly exchanged a glance and raised their eyebrows.

'After many a long year at sea, splicing mainbraces and plundering exotic islands, I have gained much knowledge and wisdom. I have seen places and people of which most folk only dream. No corner of the globe holds any surprise for me now. That is why I have made a decision. A decision that will include you two . . .'

Spot the parrot squawked indignantly.

'. . . you *three*.'

Molly and Lan Ho drew their chairs closer, with a squeak.

'For I have decided to become a detective. A pirate detective. Using all my naughty nautical knowledge for the good of our town. I shall do good deeds where once I did bad. And so will you. But what caused this sudden turn around, you may be a-thinking? What caused old Slice-'em-up Hawkins to chart a different course? This!'

And with that well-spoken speech I threw the morning paper on the breakfast table.

Molly, Lan Ho and Spot grabbed it and inspected it.

Lan Ho was the first to speak.

'*Bee-keeper Hiccups to Death*?'

'No, no,' I said irritably and snatched the paper. 'It must be mentioned in here somewhere.' I finally found the report and held it up for all to see.

Molly read slowly.

'*Priceless Cut-glass Cutlass stolen from town museum. Curator in tears.*'

Lan Ho, Molly and Spot looked at me as I said, 'And we, my piratical pals, are going to find it!'

CHAPTER TWO

Molly, Ho and I stood before the museum, which sat on the edge of the town square. Washed-upon-the-Beach was a fine old seaport, its history dating back hundred of years. It was founded in the fifth century AD by St Figgy, patron saint of tadpoles. Now a few seagulls circled over the museum entrance and sunlight danced off its dirty windows. Therein lay our destiny and our future. We all took a deep breath and headed for the main doors.

At the reception desk the man I recognized from the televisual machine looked up nervously.

'Good afternoon, ladies and gentlemen. And welcome to the Washed-upon-the-Beach Museum.

I am the curator, Horace Silk. We have a fine display of seafaring trivia. From a stuffed mermaid to Admiral Nelson's famous log and some of his less famous twigs. Sadly, though, our prize exhibit is no longer with us . . .' he sniffed slightly, '. . .the Mayor is devastated.'

'And that is where I can help you,' I announced proudly, 'for I am none other than Sam Hawkins, Pirate Detective. I am the private pirate detective for the whole of Washed-upon-the-Beach. This is my private eye patch!'

Horace Silk looked at us strangely and scratched his ear. He nibbled his pencil and fingered his rubber stamp.

'How intriguing. How can I help you?'

Molly stepped forward and thumped the desk-bell, squashing it with her mighty fist.

'No, we help you. Got it?'

I intervened before she could inflict any more help.

'Yes, curator, I have come to solve your crime. Show us to the scene, please.'

'But the police have already been and investigated, thank you,' he sighed.

'Have they?'

'Yes.'

'Oh.'

I fiddled with my neckerchief and tried a different way to get in.

'How much is a ticket?'

'Two pounds each.'

And here was our first problem. None of us had any money. Curses and blubber! How were we to solve the case of the Cut-glass Cutlass if we couldn't even get to the scene of the crime?

'Two pounds *each*,' he repeated, a little more insistently.

'Yes, yes, I heard you,' I said. 'Do these look like a deaf man's ears?'

Horace Silk seemed unsure of an answer.

CRASH!

His attention was suddenly drawn to a chattering gaggle of school children who tumbled into the foyer, accompanied by a hassled-looking teacher.

'Fiona, take that out of your ear . . . Martin, don't squeeze it . . . Holly, put it down very gently . . . George, don't even think about it.'

They were drawn to the reception desk like hungry goldfish to the surface of a pond.

'How many?' asked Horace.

'Twenty,' replied the teacher.

A small child corrected her. 'Nineteen, miss.'

'Why nineteen, Timmy?'

'Because Nigel was sick on his cat, remember?'

'Oh, yes, nineteen then, please!'

The teacher handed over the cash and Horace counted the party through. 'Nineteen . . . twenty . . . twenty-one . . . twentytwo.'

He stopped and thought. 'Excuse me, miss, there appears to be . . .'

But the teacher couldn't hear him. She was already inside the museum.

And so were we!

The town museum was a dark, dank place and smelt like the bilges of a schooner after a particularly long voyage. The first corridor was filled with stuffed animals, all frozen in poses. A large blue whale dominated one room we passed and to its left were some manky-looking penguins with patches. In fact, every room seemed to have some stuffed creature in it.

Now, if I were still in the pirate trade this would be the perfect place to hide treasure. The reason? No one ever seemed to come here. Lonely exhibits sat behind dirty glass – here a fish, there a fish, everywhere another fish, a couple of anchors and a few broken rum bottles. Finally, at the end of the hallway, was a sign:

TO THE CUT-GLASS CUTLASS

and scribbled below were the words

Exhibit Temporarily Stolen

'What's the plan, boss?' said Molly, picking something from her teeth.

Before I could speak, Lan Ho produced a strange mechanical object from under his jacket.

'What's that?' I asked, pointing at it.

'You are so out of touch, Sam Hawkins!' he sneered sweetly. 'It's a video camera, dumbo!'

I wished he'd find a new nickname for me.

'Off you go then,' I sighed. 'And Molly, you go and . . . well, ermm . . . find some clues.'

'OK, boss,' and she stumbled off into the shadows.

But what was I to do? How was I to make my debut in the world of detection?

It was at this point that I heard voices. One soft and mumbling, the other much harsher. I pressed my ear to a door marked 'Cleaning Fluids', but there was nothing there. Next 'Filing Cabinets'. Still nothing. But when I suddenly saw a door marked 'Private – Curator's Office. Wait to be invited', I knew I'd found the source of the sounds.

I placed my ear against the door and this is what I heard.

'Private detective?' said the sharp voice.

'Yes, I'm afraid so, Lola . . .'

'Don't call me Lola, Horace. To you I am the Mayor and you should be grateful I'm visiting your pokey little museum!'

'Oh, I am, but this detective might be able to help find the Cut-glass Cutlass.'

'We don't need a private detective – we have a perfectly good police force at work as we speak! Now get out!'

Footsteps approached the door. I leaped over to a plant stand and hid behind it. The door of the office was flung open and out scuttled Horace Silk.

He saw me crouching behind the stand. What could I say?

'Morning, Mr Silk. Isn't this a nice plant stand. Look at the way those legs reach the floor . . .'

The curator said nothing and scurried off down the corridor.

'Do you like flowers, Mr Hawkins?'

The voice came from the doorway. I turned and there was a female of bewitching beauty, a staggering smile on her lips and a playful glint in her eye. The vision spoke.

'Hi, I'm the Mayor, Lola Schwartz!'

'I'm Sam Hawkins . . .'

'Pirate Detective. Yes, I heard. You want a drink?'

She took my hand and led me into the office, closing the door behind her.

The sunlight squeezed its way through the blinds at the window and on the desk a small fan threw out cool air. A coffee machine plopped in the background.

'Coffee?' she asked.

'Tea would be nice,' I replied.

She leaned forward.

'*Coffee?*'

'Coffee would be nice, too.'

She sauntered over to the coffee machine and started to pour.

'Twas a grotty little office, just like the rest of the museum. Dirty brown filing cabinets, yellow walls and some dusty files. To one side an ancient, heavily dented photocopier was straining away at its duties.

'Looks like you could do with a new copier!' I said, playfully making conversation. The Mayor glanced across at it as it wheezed out another sheet of paper.

'I know. Looks like someone sat on it!' she said, pouring the coffee. 'So what brings you to our little museum – sugar?'

I went red. No one had called me sugar before. Certainly no maid as beautiful as the Mayor.

'Well, sweetie . . .' I said, fingering my collar.

The Mayor stopped pouring.

'Why did you call me sweetie?'

'Cos you called me sugar.'

'I was asking you if you wanted sugar in your coffee!'

I went red again. I tried to think of something to say. Lola stirred my coffee. Clink, clink.

'Why the interest in the museum?' she asked. 'No crimes at sea? No lost catfish? No one mug a halibut?'

I shifted uncomfortably in the chair.

'I've only recently taken to detecting, ma'am. I've put away my sea legs and am now solving crimes.'

'How generous of you.' She placed the coffee before me.

Suddenly a loud alarm exploded in our ears. Lola ran for the door. I followed close behind.

The alarm stopped as suddenly as it had started.

'What in the bluest of blue brinies is a-going on?' I cried as we ran into the Cutlass Room.

What a sight befell my eyes!

At one side of the room was a dusty hammerhead shark. Underneath it was Lan Ho, holding his videoing machine. On the other side of the room stood Molly, clutching in her huge hands a small, screaming child. Behind her was a large broken window.

As the alarm stopped, everyone froze.

My eagle eyes darted about. 'Twas a big, light room in the centre of which was a large plinth. A large, empty plinth. A small card next to it read 'Cut-glass Cutlass', but 'twas, of course, no longer there. The room seemed sad without it.

The curator scurried in.

'What have you done to my museum?' he screeched.

'Explain yourselves,' demanded Lola.

We pulled Lan Ho from under the shark.

'I'm all right! I'm all right!'

'But what happened?' I said, brushing down my little pal.

He slapped my hand away, then took a deep breath. 'I was trying to get some good shots of the room. So I climbed on to the shark. But it went all wobbly and crashed.'

Molly stepped forward, the small child swinging from her hand. The teacher was tugging at her massive arm with little effect. Molly ignored her cries.

'I've done better than that, boss. Look . . .' Molly pointed with the child. 'What do you see?'

'Will you please release Mortimer?' demanded the schoolteacher.

We looked at the floor of the room. All about us were small footprints. No bigger than the footprints of . . .

'A small child!' Molly announced. 'So I went and got one to see if they fitted. He struggled a bit, so I had to swing him around to get him to concentrate. But then I broke a window with his head and the alarm went off.'

'It hurt a lot, actually!' said Mortimer, dangling upside down.

'You broke my window!' said the curator, wagging a finger at the inverted child.

'Will you please release this boy!' insisted the teacher, poking Molly's thigh.

But I heard no more of the argument – my sharp eye was suddenly drawn towards an interesting object on the ground. I dropped to my knees and shuffled closer. Below the broken window, next to a small footprint, was a red herring. How had a red herring – a fish usually seen in water – found its way on to dry land and into the museum? And did these footprints really belong to this child? I was shaken from my thoughts by the voice of another small child.

'Look, miss, I found somebody's bottom! It was underneath the shark!'

A little girl was holding up a creased piece of paper on which was clearly photocopied a naked human bottom. The teacher snatched the sheet from the girl and stared at it, her face turning a violent shade of pink.

'Come along, class, let's go and see the seaweed exhibition!'

She slapped the mysterious photocopy into my hand and herded the children from the room.

I heard a final voice as they disappeared down the corridor.

'But I want my bottom back!' I inspected the strange posterior. The child was right. 'Twas a bottom, and a spotty one, too. And on one cheek was a tattoo. A tattoo of a curly anchor. Who would want an anchor on their bottom, I wondered?

Mr Silk looked at the mess in the room and then slowly turned to me. 'The police must have missed that. Some wretched fellow has clearly broken into the museum and not only stolen our precious Cut-glass Cutlass, but also chosen to taunt us with his bottom. I shall be a laughing stock at the next curators' tea party!' He blew his nose.

'But what about this!' I said, waving the fish at him.

'Oh, that – that's just a red herring!'

☠   ☠

As we sailed into harbour back at the Naughty Lass we were all a little silent. Our first day of detecting had not been a huge success, but we had gathered some clues – the red herring, the footprints and a photocopied bottom with a tattoo of a curly anchor. I looked up at the painting of my mother. It was a beautiful portrait. Wherever you walked in the room her nose seemed to follow you.

'You're going to be proud of me, Mother,' I said, softly. 'I'll get back the Cut-glass Cutlass. I promise.'

CHAPTER THREE

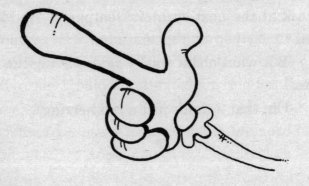

The next day all was quiet aboard the Naughty Lass. Our first voyage into the grimy waters of crime and we hadn't netted one single slippery robber. This detecting business was proving a lot tougher than we had thought. After a hearty breakfast of something yellow on toast we moved into the lounge to discuss the case.

'Hic!'

'Zzzzzzzz!'

'Hic!'

'Zzzzzzzz!'

Molly and Ho were all a-slumber as soon as the meeting started. Molly was snoring in her sleep and Ho was hiccuping in his. I sat in my armchair, twiddling my salty thumbs and wondering what to do next.

My barnacled brain tussled with the clues we had unearthed at the museum. I stared down at the evidence on the wonky coffee table. How had a small red herring (slightly nibbled, I noticed) come to be in the museum? Judging from its smell, it had been out of water for a while. And what about the footprints of the small child? Thoughts and ideas swished and swoshed through my brain.

And then there were the Washed-upon-the-Beach police. Were they hot on the fins of our criminal? Were they piecing together the flotsam and jetsam of the clues? Were they preparing to plunge into the heart of the underworld and drag out our culprit? Oh, slop buckets! Old Sam Hawkins was not going to be capsized on his first voyage! I wasn't going to allow the police to win this race – I needed to fire up my crew!

I leaped to my feet, strode over to the fireplace and donged the ship's bell loudly. Lan Ho and Molly muttered and mumbled as they dragged themselves from their snooze. I gazed out over my crew and launched into a speech.

'Friends, pirates, midshipmen . . .'

'And women!' interrupted Molly, waving her pipe at me.

'. . . and women. Now is the time to combine our skills, to nail our colours to the rigging, to put our noses to the ground and our ears to the grindstone. Let us squeeze every drop from our nautical experience and solve this confuddling mystery!'

Lan Ho shook his head as if coming out of hypnosis and Molly sat up straight.

I carefully picked up the red herring, held it to my nose and sniffed it.

'How does it smell, boss?' asked Ho.

'Fishy, very fishy. But the question is – how did it get into the museum? And, secondly, who nibbled it?'

Molly spoke.

'Maybe it was kidnapped!'

She jumped to her feet and straightened her kilt.

'That's it!' she said enthusiastically. 'The herring was kidnapped by an evil fisherman and somewhere, below the waves, a sad mummy herring pines for her lost child . . .'

She began pacing back and forth.

'And the evil fisherman has written a ransom note, put it in a bottle, tied it to a rock or maybe . . .' she paused smugly, '. . . a brick, and thrown it into the sea!'

She looked at Lan Ho for a reaction. Lan Ho sighed and looked at me for a reaction. I was about to speak when Molly started to applaud herself. She glared at me and Ho and waited.

'Well done, Molly!' we said.

'Molly,' I said, 'if this red herring has been kidnapped, as you suggest, and this evil fisherman is holding it to ransom, what, in the blithering blue blazes, is it doing here?'

Molly slowly sat back down.

'Perhaps it fell out of his pocket,' she said weakly.

The room fell silent. I turned the fish back and forth in my hand. My eyes drifted over to the photocopied bottom from the museum. Suddenly, something about it caught my eye and I leapt over to inspect it more closely.

Next to the bottom was something I hadn't noticed before, though my well-trained piratical eye can spy a shark leagues away. Just visible in the picture was a photocopy of a hand. A gnarled and weathered old hand it was, too. And there was writing on the palm of the hand. You probably do it yourself – write a note to yourself on your hand so you don't forget something: 'Do homework', 'Wash the hedgehog', 'Hide the jam', that kind of thing. But what this note said, my eagle eye couldn't tell. The writing was too small.

'Molly – how would you make a bottom bigger?'

'Cream cakes' she said quietly.

Pah! Some use she was. I found my magnifying glass and looked again. This is what I saw:

sta sh Cut-glas s Cut las s at Benbo w rec

Lan Ho grabbed the magnifying glass and peered closely.

'That's not English, Sam!'

He stared at the words for a few minutes then made some pencil marks on the paper. 'Duh! It's obvious!' He grinned. I looked again. A phrase had emerged. This is what I saw:

stash Cut-glass Cutlass at Benbo wrec

'Twas obvious what had happened! When our criminal photocopied his (or her) bottom he'd (or she'd) accidentally photocopied his (or her) hand – a hand with a telltale clue upon it. It all made sense . . . except the last two words.

'The wreck of the *Benbo*!' Ho suddenly shouted, jumping up and frightening the parrot. 'The K didn't copy!'

The boy was a genius!

'*Benbo* wreck.' I mulled the words over and over, but I was still flummoxed. 'I've never heard of the wreck of the *Benbo*. Have you?'

Molly racked her brains. It didn't take long.

'No,' she admitted.

''Tis time, then, for a little research. Ho – man the encyclopedias! Molly – hoist the maps!'

And with that the salty crew of the Naughty Lass set to work, pouring over every inch of every chart and every book we owned. Ho burrowed from A to Z, page after page. Molly spun the globe time and time again. I, however, took the task of making the tea – keeping the crew well fuelled was a vital job and I took great care not to leave the tea bags in too long.

'I've found a wreck!' Ho suddenly announced. 'And it's right here in Washed-upon-the-Beach!'

I bounded over to the book he was reading.

'HMS *Gibbering* went down, with twenty-seven hands and twenty-six feet, off the coast of Washed-upon-the-Beach in 1893!'

'Of course, Great Uncle Tweaker told me of that tragedy!' I said.

'Was he on board?' asked Molly.

'He pulled the plug out! But that's not the *Benbo* wreck, Ho, that's the *Gibbering* wreck!'

We set sail on our research once again, but all to no avail.

Pooped and unable to focus any further, we flopped in a heap on the settee.

'Well, there's no *Benbo* wreck!' said Ho.

Molly nodded in agreement. 'Doesn't exist.'

I looked up at the painting of my mother. I wondered what she'd do in this situation. Have a glass of gin, probably.

We settled for a mug of cocoa.

CHAPTER FOUR

'Cock-a-doodle-doooooo!'

It was that fiddling and faddling parrot. 'Twas five o'clock in the morning and I was lying in my hammock being woken by a parrot doing cockerel impressions. Spot had taken to imitating other animals ever since we'd worked on a chicken farm. We didn't last long at that job. I think I must have been planting them too deep.

'Cock-a-doodle-doooooo!'

I'd tied my hammock to the posts of my four-poster bed. Can't get used to a landlubber's bed, y'see. They don't move enough. I carefully disembarked, adjusting my nightshirt as I did so.

I threw back the curtains and gazed at the wonderful town of Washed-upon-the-Beach spread out before me. Even the dustbins seemed to be smiling in the sunlight. Down in the garden stood Molly and Ho. I couldn't hear a word they were saying, but their body language told me they were having an argument. I detected this by the way Molly was holding Ho by the neck and tugging at his hair. Barnacles! A captain couldn't have an upset crew. I headed towards the garden.

'No, no, no!' screamed Ho. 'You're wrong!'

'No! You're wrong!' bellowed Molly.

Ho pushed his fingers in his ears and chanted, 'Wrong, wrong, wrong, wrong, wrong!'

I looked at the situation and tried to decide what to do. Should I thrust myself between them and force them apart or shout at them until they stopped?

'Stop fighting!' I shouted as I stomped into the garden.

Molly dropped Ho like a cannonball and he collapsed in a heap. 'Whatever is going on? You look like you've been up all night!'

'We have,' yawned Molly. 'All because of her,' said Ho, rubbing his elbow.

'But why?' Ho hopped to his feet, ambled over to the green fishpond and snatched a small paper boat from the surface.

'We been working on the case, actually, Sam!'

He handed me the soggy newspaper boat.

'See this model of the boat . . .'

'What boat?'

'The boat the herring was sailing, of course.' He rolled his eyes at me.

'Herrings don't sail boats!' I was starting to get confused.

'See!' Molly shouted triumphantly, and glared at Ho, who squirmed slightly.

I looked at the soggy mass in my hand.

'Is this today's paper?'

'Yes, it just came through the letter box.'

I unfolded it gently. Suddenly my eyes fell on something fascinating.

'Look at that!' I said, stabbing the paper and handing it to Ho.

Ho read, '*Tommy Atkins Wiggles His Ears for Charity!*

'No, lower down!'

'*Policeman's Socks Kidnapped!* said Molly.

I snatched back the paper and read the article that had caught my eagle eye.

'*Lady Booming-Clapshot Cleared of Receiving Stolen Goods – "I purchased my Cut-glass Cutlass in good faith!"* she said!'

'The cutlass! The cutlass!' chanted Molly and Ho, jumping up and down. (I've often wondered why people use the phrase 'jumping up and down', for it strikes me 'tis impossible to jump up *without* coming back down.)

'Then Clapshot Towers is the next destination in our search,' I proclaimed.

'Hurrah!' shouted Molly.

'And you two can stay here and tidy the Naughty Lass. I shall go alone!'

'You'd better put your breeches on then,' Ho said sulkily.

I left them giggling by the fish pond.

The sun continued to shine merrily as I tramped the two miles to Clapshot Towers, the home of Lady Elizabeth Booming-Clapshot. 'Twas a splendid building. In the good olde days Washed -upon-the-Beach was a port respected throughout the globe and populated by sailors and pirates from all four corners. I'd heard salty tales of the glorious parties held by Lady Booming-Clapshot and now was my chance to get a sneaky look at the place. But times had changed and Clapshot Towers was not what it once was. It sat unloved and unwanted like a lonely sandcastle on the outskirts of town. The house needed attention, bits were dropping off, and the building was going to seed. I realized this when the door was answered by a goat.

I doffed my hat politely when suddenly the goat disappeared and was replaced by a butler. He had a face like a used tea bag with a wig on. He eyed me suspiciously.

'What do you want?' he snapped, accidently spitting out his false teeth and deftly catching them again. He quickly replaced them and said, 'Tradesmen's entrance!' and slammed the big red door in my face.

At the tradesmen's entrance I tugged at the bell-pull and heard a distant tinkle deep inside the mansion.

The door swung open and the butler's head popped out.

'I am Whithers the Butler,' he snapped. 'What do you want?'

'I am Sam Hawkins, Pirate Detective, and I'm investigating the case of the Cut-glass Cutlass.'

'You're not a tradesman, then?'

'No!'

'Then why are you using the tradesmen's entrance? Go round to the front!' he sneered, and slammed the door.

Back at the front door I reached out for the bellpull, but the door opened before I could ring it.

Whithers's face emerged like a tortoise coming out of its shell.

'Don't pull that!' he snapped. 'You'll ring the bell! Come inside.'

He threw open the door and I followed him in.

I've supped soup with kings and queens and guzzled coffee with senators. I've even played tiddlywinks with an archduke, but none of their homes compared to the boggling sight I encountered as I stepped across the threshold of Clapshot Towers.

'Twas a tatty old place, but still had remnants of the splendour of old. So the tales were true. The hall was the size of a cricket pitch and festooned with paintings of long-dead ancestors. The floor was highly polished and suits of rusty armour stood sentry against the walls. I gazed about and could almost hear the sound of distant waltzes and the lost laughter of years ago. I was dragged from my dream by the butler saying, 'Keyring?'

I turned to see a small table on which were various tourist flotsam and jetsam. All had the words 'Clapshot Towers' on them.

'Or a nice T-shirt, perhaps? How about a stick of Clapshot rock?'

I politely declined the butler's offer. He went all huffy.

'Wait here,' he ordered. I was about to reply when he suddenly produced a small trumpet from inside a grandfather clock and gave it a hefty blast.

The report echoed through the hundreds of corridors and we waited in silence.

'Her ladyship will be down presently,' said Whithers.

The silence was suddenly shattered by a squeal of delight.

'Guests! Little darling guests!'

I looked up the huge staircase and there stood Lady Booming-Clapshot, looking like a slightly deflated bouncy castle. The sunlight glinted off her tiara as she descended, waving majestically.

At which point two police officers appeared behind her. One tall and thin and male, the other short and fat and female.

'Madam, please, all we need is one tiny peek at the cutlass to make sure that . . .' said the policewoman, trailing after her ladyship.

'Enough, enough! Thank you, Officer Stump, thank you, Officer Stibbins, but you're ruining my entrance. Run along now!'

'Well, we'll come and inspect it later, then!' said the female of the pair.

As her ladyship descended she began to talk to me. Well, I say me – she sounded like she was addressing Parliament.

'Dear, dear friends, honoured fellows, lords, ladies and gentlemen. It is a pleasure to greet you all and welcome each and every one of you to my humble home!'

Seeing their task was hopeless, the police trotted down the stairs behind her, replacing their hats, and headed for the large brown door.

'Good morning, sir!' they muttered to me. 'Call me Hawkins,' I said, pulling up the collar of my coat. 'Sam Hawkins!'

The police officers stopped and turned to me.

'The Pirate Detective?' 'The same!' I shrugged, trying to look moody and tough.

The two officers giggled and ran out of the door. I'd obviously impressed them.

Suddenly Lady Booming-Clapshot was at my side. She put on her glasses. Her face dropped.

'Just the one, Whithers?'

'Just the one, your ladyship,' nodded the butler.

She held my hand, sighed deeply and shook it. She looked intently into my eyes, but spoke to the butler.

'Have you sold any souvenirs, Whithers?' she asked.

'Not one, my lady,' he replied, inspecting his nails.

Her ladyship lowered her voice.

'Poor old Whithers. The only money he makes is from selling souvenirs. Whithers has ten children — all they've had to eat this week is a marrow.'

I plunged my hand into my pocket and pulled out two pounds. I handed it to him grudgingly and took an 'I ♥ Clapshot Towers' badge.

'How splendid to have you here today,' she announced. 'I do hope you enjoy your short visit to Clapshot Towers. I shall arrange for Whithers to give you a guided tour later.'

'Oh, piddle,' said the butler, but her ladyship chose not to hear.

'It is a wonderful home. A wonderful, wonderful home.' She looked about the hall wistfully. 'I haven't changed a thing since my darling hubby, Admiral Booming-Clapshot, was lost at sea all those years ago.'

She stopped suddenly.

'Whithers! Dab me!'

Whithers shuffled forward, pulled a stained handkerchief from his pocket and gently wiped a tear from her cheek.

'But anyway, how can we help you?' her ladyship continued.

'I am Sam Hawkins, Pirate Detective, and I am investigating the case of the stolen Cut-glass Cutlass.'

Whithers and her ladyship exchanged a shifty glance.

'Well, it's been delightful meeting you. Do call again. Whithers, the door.' And with that, Lady Booming- Clapshot hitched up her dress and started to make off down the hall.

I had to think quickly. I couldn't let her leave so soon. An idea emerged from the depths of my mind and I took the plunge.

'Did you say you were married to Admiral Booming-Clapshot?'

Lady Booming-Clapshot halted mid-scurry. She turned slowly.

'Did you know him?'

'Indeed, I did,' I said, smiling my most charming smile. She wasn't to know Admiral Booming-Clapshot was the most unable seaman ever to weigh anchor. I'd only heard of him by word of mouth, but many said he was the worst sailor at sea.

'Finest sailor at sea,' I said, smiling.

'Can you stay for lunch?' she asked.

The butler groaned.

The dining room was vast. I could have built a galleon in the space and still had room to net a whale. Not only was it vast, 'twas also dark and dreary. I looked around, inspecting its awesomeness.

'Why are the curtains closed?'

I asked. Her ladyship touched the edge of a curtain and said slowly, 'I shall never open another curtain until my darling hubby, Albert, returns.'

'Fair enough,' I said, continuing to look about.

The table, which could easily seat fifty diners, was in the centre of the dining room. Whithers gestured grumpily towards my seat at one end, then took her ladyship's arm and walked her to the other.

He seated her gently and disappeared. Lady Booming-Clapshot unfurled a napkin and shouted, 'So where did you meet dear Albert?'

I leaned back in my chair and launched into a tale. ''Twas in my days aboard the good ship Scuttle Butt. We had just plundered a small island and were making good our escape . . .'

'Was he handsome then?'

'Oh, very handsome . . . and we was ploughing at a rate of knots towards open water. Before us hoved into view HMS *Seaworthy* . . .'

'My hubby's ship,' she squealed, strangling her napkin.

'Indeed . . . and we . . .'

'Was it as beautiful as I remember it?'

'The ship? Yes, beautiful ship. Lovely round portholes . . . and then we sneakily pulled down our Jolly Roger as it drew closer, and at that moment . . .'

The door banged open and in shuffled Whithers, pushing a squeaking trolley. On it was a large dish covered with a silver lid. He pushed the trolley towards her ladyship's end of the table, parked it by her and whispered in her ear. Her ladyship nodded and said,'Good point, Whithers.'

She banged the salt cellar on the table.

'Mr Hawkins, it has just occurred to me to ask you something. What precisely are you doing here?'

'Twas obvious I was never going to finish my salty sea tale, so I abandoned the story and answered her question.

'Well, your ladyship, I have certain information gathered from this very morning's paper that you have come into possession of the Cut-glass Cutlass.'

Whithers slowly took the dish from the trolley and placed it before her ladyship. He didn't take his pokey eyes off me.

'Hogswash and pigswill,' she said suddenly, then smiled sweetly, 'as my husband used to say. Remove the lid, Whithers.'

Whithers removed the lid, revealing a cake which, compared to Ho's cooking, looked succulent.

'I have recently purchased a new addition to my art collection, that is true. And it is, indeed, a Cutglass Cutlass, but I can assure you, Mr Hawkins, it is not the Cut-glass Cutlass.' She rearranged her cutlery. 'I intend to display it in the West Wing to attract more visitors. It may not be obvious to you, Mr Hawkins, but our income is very low at the moment.'

'I must see this cutlass!' I demanded.

'Whithers – fetch the cutlass!'

Whithers bowed slightly and, with a groan, left the room.

'Your morning paper, Mr Hawkins, is full of fiddlefaddle and tittle-tattle!'

I paced back and forth.

'Perhaps so, your ladyship, but until my detective mind is satisfied this is not the cutlass I seek, I shall not rest!'

'Pish and tush, if you ask me,' she muttered, polishing a spoon.

At that moment the door swung open at the far end of the room and in stepped Whithers, carrying before him a thin, narrow box wrapped in red felt. He shuffled towards our end of the table.

'Hurry, man, hurry – if this is the cutlass I seek . . .'

'Which it's not,' said her ladyship. 'Allow me to disappoint you, Mr Hawkins – this is my Cut-glass Cutlass.'

She opened the lid of the box and we all peered in. What we saw took the wind from all our sails.

The box was empty!

'Whithers, where's my cutlass?'

The butler seemed genuinely surprised and he continued gaping at the box.

'But . . . but . . . but . . .' he stammered, 'I placed it there myself this morning. It's been stolen!'

'Barnacles!' I cursed, and smacked my fist on the table.

'But it's worth a fortune!' squealed her ladyship.

Realizing what she'd said, the butler and her ladyship fell silent and looked like naughty oysters.

'So it was the *real* Cut-glass Cutlass?' I said.

'Oh, well,' said Whithers. He undid his bow tie, slipped his wig from his head and fanned himself with it.

'Yes, yes, it was the *real* Cut-glass Cutlass!' he admitted. 'Her ladyship bought it with a stash of cash left to tide her over until her hubby's return . . . Oh, don't sniff . . . and was hoping to use it to attract more visitors.'

'But I don't understand. How did you get it? Did you steal it from the museum?'

'No, no, we were contacted by an anonymous seller.'

'Absolutely fascinating.' I inspected the box more closely. 'And so is this! Look what I've found!' I waved a nibbled red herring before her ladyship's face.

It was obviously the final straw. She suddenly exploded.

'Leave at once! Get out of my home and never return, you blithering blackguard! If only my husband were here he'd challenge you to a duel. Whithers, challenge him to a duel!'

Whithers was glumly drumming a dessert spoon on the table

'Oh, shut up, woman!' he muttered.

Her ladyship was red with anger.

'Leave at once and take your herring with you!' she bellowed. 'Whithers, see this man to the door, then come back and dab me!'

I realized I'd pushed matters a little too far and started reversing out of the room, bowing and apologizing at the same time. I left her ladyship sniffling her tears into the butler's lapel.

I made off down the driveway, my new clue safely in my pocket, and hardly heard the door slam behind me.

CHAPTER FIVE

What bubbling bounty I had in my salty palm! A second red herring (also nibbled). Bit by bit I was netting every clue in this mysterious case. But questions still bobbed about in my briny brain.

What was the meaning of these little red herrings?

Where was the wreck of the BENBO?

Who had written the message on their hand?

Whose bottom was it?

Who was the stranger who sold the cutlass to Lady Booming-Clapshot?

Who kept stealing it?

I hurried back to the Naughty Lass, eager to show my discovery to my shipmates. As I turned the corner of Puddle Lane, a shocking sight met my eyes. On the front lawn, tied to the flagpole, was Spot the Parrot, a white mask across his little eyes and a small banana on his head.

I stopped by the fence and took in the sight.

At the other end of the lawn Molly was standing giggling, and in her hand was her bow. She placed an arrow in it, slowly brought it up to her eye and aimed at Spot. I leaped over the fence and landed between her and the parrot.

'Heave-ho!' I bellowed. 'What is a-happening and why has that parrot got a banana on its head?'

Molly lowered the bow. 'I couldn't find an apple,' she explained. 'Shift now, boss.'

'You can't do this – 'tis but a poor helpless parrot.'

Lan Ho appeared from behind Molly's bulky body, holding his catapult. He'd obviously been having a go, too.

'It's only target practice!' he said, with his hands on his hips. 'It might come in handy one day!'

'Well, stop it at once. This parrot has been my seafaring companion for many a long year.' I began untying Spot. 'The japes and scrapes we have shared together will go down in history. I saved this parrot from the evil clutches of Captain "Oily" Wragg, who'd trained him to peck jewels from the crowns of lords and ladies who sailed aboard his *Thieving Magpie*. He's been my faithful companion from that day to this.'

Spot threw his wings around me.

'No need to be *that* faithful!' I said, tugging him from my neck.

Molly reluctantly removed the arrow from her bow and thrust it into the quiver slung across her back.

'I could have been a great archer, you know,' she said sadly.

She stomped back into the Naughty Lass, leaving Ho staring at me, twanging his catapult crossly.

'I try and organize a bit of staff training and this is the thanks I get! Why ever I had to be rescued by you I'll never know. It could have been the Emperor of China, you know.'

'Inside!'

Spot threw his wings about my head and began pecking my ear gratefully.

Inside the living room Molly was sulking in the tatty armchair and slapping through the pages of *Jackie Tar*.

I entered the room, trying to tug Spot from my shoulder.

'Go to your perch!' I ordered.

Spot obeyed eagerly. I strode over to the ship's bell and gave it three hearty rings.

'Crew meeting! Crew meeting!' I bellowed. Ho ambled into the room and Molly put aside her magazine. Whilst I had their concentration I launched into my account of the fascinating events at Clapshot Towers.

'And now,' I announced proudly, 'I have hatched a plan whereby we shall trawl the whole of Clapshot Towers for further clues.'

'She won't let you back in, I bet,' said Molly.

'Ah-ha!' I said triumphantly, 'that is the clever part of my plan. She won't know I've returned. For I shall go back – in the dead of night!'

I donged the bell once more and Spot squawked.

'And you lot are coming, too!'

☠   ☠

On the stroke of midnight three dark shadows slunk out of the Naughty Lass and along Puddle Lane. One smaller shadow fluttered behind.

'Twas not long before we found ourselves outside Clapshot Towers. A single candle flickered in a window high above, and we could just make out the silhouette of Lady Booming-Clapshot. My maritime training had taught me all about the art of night-time manoeuvres. We were all wearing black balaclavas and black bin liners. They did rustle a bit, though.

'Right, crew,' I whispered, as we huddled behind a bush. 'Let's check our equipment.'

'Check our equipment!' squawked Spot in my ear.

I clasped my hand across his beak.

'One more word from your blinking beak,' I hissed, 'and you'll walk the plank.'

Spot gulped and fell silent.

Molly took the sack from her shoulder and placed it on the ground.

'Torches?' I asked.

'Torches,' she confirmed, handing them out.

'Crowbar?'

'Scissors?'

'Plastic bags?'

'String?'

'Sam?' enquired Ho. 'Whatever are we going to need string for?'

I placed a solemn hand on his young shoulders and said, 'You never know what terrors may lie before us, Lan Ho.'

'Look!' Molly hissed, pointing at the window high above.

The silhouette of Lady Booming-Clapshot had stopped moving. My heart missed a beat. We held our breath.

The candle went out and we breathed again.

'Give her a few minutes to get off to sleep and we'll make good our entry.'

Those few minutes took an eternity to pass, but finally we found ourselves by a small, ground-floor window at the rear of Clapshot Towers. Lan Ho slid in his crowbar and, with the merest of creaks, the window swung open. We clambered inside. Ha! Every clue we needed to solve this puzzling crime would soon be in our clammy grasp. But which room had we entered?

There was a splash and then silence.

'My foot's wet,' whispered Molly.

I switched on a torch and scanned the small room. A mirror, a towel, a sink, a roll of toilet paper . . . oh dear . . .

'This is why we are well equipped,' I said. I pulled out a plastic bag, dropped to my knees, extracted Molly's foot from the toilet bowl, placed it in the bag and sealed it up with string.

'And now,' I said firmly, 'to work.'

The hallway outside the toilet was long and narrow and stank of cleaning fluids. The tiniest noise seemed to echo through the building.

'What exactly are we looking for?' whispered Molly, squelching slightly.

'I'll tell you when we find it,' I explained. 'Split up and investigate.'

We rummaged through the whole of Clapshot Towers. We ransacked and rifled every room. We combed every corner and scoured every section. We turned Clapshot Towers upside down, inside out and back to front. We searched high and low, and low and high. But not one single, solitary clue could we find.

A whole hour later we gathered in the front hall.

'Blast my cannons!' I cursed softly. 'There must be something here. Just one single sign of do -baddery!'

At this point, Spot bit my ear. I shrieked loudly and Molly clasped a firm hand over my mouth to silence me. 'Twas too late – the shriek bounced off the walls and echoed down the corridors.

We sat as still as a millpond, no one daring to breathe.

Slowly it dawned on us that the shriek had not been heard by anyone but us. We were safe.

'What,' I hissed at Spot, 'did you do that for?'

Spot grabbed my hand in his claws and started to flap off down a shadowy corridor we hadn't noticed before. We had trouble keeping up.

Eventually he stopped, perched himself on top of a suit of armour and nodded towards a door. I slid a torch from my pocket and switched it on. A polished brass plaque hung on the door. Ho read slowly:

'Albert's Memorial

memories of my dear husband,

Admiral Albert Booming-Clapshot.

£2 entrance fee in the box, please.'

'Twas a room none of us had plundered. But what lay beyond?

I gently pushed the door and it creaked open quietly. We stepped inside.

In the darkness our three torches scanned the room. It was festooned with every trinket and treasure connected with Admiral Booming-Clapshot. To the left was a painting of him collecting a trophy. Ho shuffled towards it and read the caption: 'For services to Frog Hunting.'

Next to that was a black and white photograph of him dressed in arctic expedition gear. The caption read: 'Albert goes in search of the West Pole.'

There were certificates for sailing and a picture of him doing the long jump. He was certainly a heroic man, and he looked like a well-polished anchor. We inspected the bits and bobs of his history, but none gave us a clue as to the whereabouts of the Cut-glass Cutlass.

Then, in the centre of the room, we saw a small mahogany table in the middle of which was a box. The same box that Whithers the butler had set before her ladyship that very afternoon. I swallowed slightly and moved towards it. Had the Cut-glass Cutlass really been stolen, as her ladyship claimed, or were we on the brink of discovering it?

The torches of Molly and Ho lit my way as I placed my hand on the box and threw open the lid. I stared inside.

Lan Ho came over and stared with me.

'It's an empty box, Sam. Can we go home now?'

I grimaced at Spot, who was merrily hopping from claw to claw on my shoulder. I pointed my poking finger at him.

'Why did you bring us here, then, you stupid bird?'

'Look, boss!' Molly was on her hands and knees. 'An impression of a shoe.'

'This is no time to show off your party tricks, Molly!'

'No, no, I mean footprints – all over the place, little footprints.'

We scanned the floor with our torches. Molly was right. All about us were the prints of tiny feet. And they were muddy footprints, too. Some roguish rapscallion had a heart of stone to lure young children into a world of crime. He must be stopped. Or at least made to teach them to wipe their feet properly.

'Sam, look what I've got.'

Lan Ho had gathered a handful of red herrings.

'Then there's no doubt about it, me hearties,' I said sternly. 'This crime was perpetrated by the selfsame slimy smuggler who snaffled the Cutlass from the museum!'

I patted Spot on the head.

'Now to return to the Naughty Lass!'

'Wait a minute, boss.'

Molly nodded over towards a curtain that was moving very slowly back and forth.

I gulped.

Molly, gallant hero that she was, bounded over, threw back the curtain and yelled, 'Come out, you yellow-bellied jellyfish!'

But no one was there.

Only an open window – through which a gentle breeze was blowing the curtain back and forth.

Molly was soon peering at the window frame through her magnifying glass. I joined her.

'What have you spied?'

She pointed and I looked more closely. Wedged betwixt the frame and the window was a small piece of pink card. Somebody had used it to hold open the window. Perhaps the very same person who'd committed the crime.

'There she blows! Well done, Moll. Now, very carefully . . .'

Before I had time to finish my sentence, Molly snatched the card and smiled broadly.

'Got it!' she announced, but her words were lost as the window suddenly slammed shut, shattering and scattering glass all over the place. And windows don't shatter silently.

'You barmy barnacle – you might have woken . . .'

' . . . everyone in Clapshot Towers,' said a voice that didn't belong to Molly, Ho or me. But 'twas a voice I recognized.

Slowly, we turned and pointed our torches towards the door.

There, dressed in a tatty nightshirt, stood Whithers the butler with his wig hastily slapped on his head. In his hands he held a large, shiny shotgun. And he was pointing it at us.

'I get very grumpy when I'm woken from my sleep,' he sneered.

Smiling nervously, I began to explain. 'Ah, Whithers, I was just a-showing my colleagues around the house . . .'

'What's all this mess?' said Whithers, lowering his gun and looking about. 'Have you done this?'

'No, no, Mr Whithers – this mess was here when we arrived . . . But wait a minute. Surely you've seen it afore!'

Whithers lowered his gun further and leaned on it, looking suddenly sad.

'When I visited the Towers earlier,' I said, 'you brought out this box, so you must have been in here and seen you'd had an intruder.'

'Oh, no. You don't understand.' Whithers took a deep breath. 'I'm going to tell you something now I've never told anyone before. You see, I can't bear Admiral Booming-Clapshot. I would be pleased if he never, ever returned. Then her ladyship might finally accept my proposal of marriage. I can't bear to look at all his achievements. That's why, when I come in here, I cover my eyes.'

He put his hand over his eyes as if in pain. At this point, Spot leapt from the shadows, landed on Whithers's head and tugged at his wig. The butler beat the air with his free hand. The gun swung dangerously back and forth. Spot tore off the wig and the butler squealed. The gun dropped from his hands and he scrambled after it. The moment it hit the ground, it exploded. A nearby chandelier received the bullet, rattled loudly and crashed to the ground, dislodging a tidal wave of dust.

In the confusion we made our escape and scarpered into the night with our bin liners rustling furiously.

Far behind us in the doorway, Whithers was hastily replacing his wig and brandishing his gun.

'I'll never tell you a secret again!' he yelled.

Over my shoulder I saw candlelight in her ladyship's bedroom window.

'Breakfast time already, Whithers?' Her voice floated gently behind us as we disappeared down the road and into the moonlight.

A few miles later we stopped by a tree to catch our breath and congratulate each other on a job well done.

Molly pulled the piece of card from her tunic and we played our torches on it. The card read: 'Whackett's Circus – admit one.'

CHAPTER SIX

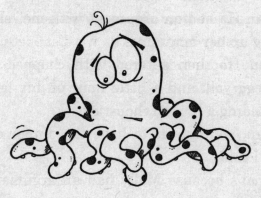

The following evening, Spot the Parrot sat on my shoulder and helped me scratch my head. What an intriguing first mystery this was proving to be. We hunched over the wonky coffee table like two grand masters of chess and considered the three clues – the red herrings, the photocopied bottom and the ticket for Whackett's Circus.

'Hmmm.' I pondered the problem.

'Hmmm!' echoed Spot.

Suddenly I heard a clattering in the kitchen. A clattering followed by a loud bang. Then Lan Ho yelled something in Chinese and Molly stumbled into the room with a wok on her head.

'Molly, my little clam, you appear to have a wok on your head,' I pointed out.

'Lan Ho had an argument with me,' she said, picking up her magazine.

Lan Ho then entered with chopped onions, some egg yolk and a little flour on his head. He was holding a broken chopstick.

'Lan, you appear to have the dinner on your head,' I said.

'That's because Molly had an argument with me. Duh!'

Now, many years at sea had taught me a thing or two about crews. Mid-voyage they get a little restless and need cheering up with a treat. I considered getting out my squeeze-box and delighting Ho and Molly with a shanty, but then another thought seized me. Supposing I was to offer them something to help the case and give them a treat? Like catching two fish with one hook.

'Crew,' I began, 'I notice from your pooped appearance and miffed attitude that you're both a little disgruntled. I have never seen a crew less gruntled, in fact. So, your good old boss has chosen to drop anchor on the case of the Cut-glass Cutlass for one evening only.'

Molly and Ho sat up and took notice.

'Harken your clam-likes as I explain. You've both worked like whales these past two days, so I have decided to grant you shore leave.'

Molly clapped her hands.

'Where we going? Where we going?'

I snatched the ticket from the coffee table.

'Whackett's Circus!' I announced.

☠   ☠

How could anyone fail to be cheered by this? I had offered my merry crew a night at the circus and topped it off with a bag of fish and chips.

'Couldn't we go to the pictures instead?' Molly asked as she dipped a chip in some chocolate sauce.

'You always want to go to the pictures!' muttered Ho, munching his haddock as he scuttled along.

'No, no, no!' I snapped. 'This circus used to be the greatest in the land and, don't forget, we found a ticket at the scene of the crime. It could be a vital clue.'

We turned a corner and there it stood – Whackett's Circus. Like a grand iceberg covered in canvas, it loomed up from the council car park overlooking the crashing, splashing sea.

We approached the ticket kiosk, where an old lady peered through a hole in a dirty window. I showed her my ticket and beckoned Molly and Ho to follow me in.

'Wait a minute,' said the little old lady. 'This only admits one.'

'And I am that one,' I replied graciously.

'And who's he?' she asked, pointing towards Lan Ho.

'He's another one.'

'One and one is two.'

'Indeed. May we enter?'

'Not without paying for another one,' she said.

'And me,' added Molly unhelpfully.

'Another two,' the little old lady demanded.

'Hogswash and pigswill!' I cursed.

I was about to launch into a speech about being an impoverished sailor without two treasure troves to rub together, when a shadow fell across my face. A large shadow, in fact, both wide and high. And from out of the shadow stepped its owner. This was not a man to be tangled with, I could tell. A huge cigar clung to his lip and smoke snaked from his mouth as he spoke.

'What's wrong, Charlene?' he asked as the smoke slithered from his mouth and up my nose. I spluttered.

'Mr Whackett, I was just asking for the entrance fee when . . .'

'Charlene, dear, go and count some money . . .'

Charlene disappeared into the depths of the kiosk and the man turned his beady eyes on us.

'I am Whackett. This is my circus. People pay to come into my circus. It costs just £5 to do so – a bargain to see some of the finest acts in the world. Tumblers, jugglers, clowns, sea lions, llamas and the world's most talented octopus. If you three wish to see my circus you must pay £15. Simple!'

I scrabbled around in my purse, mumbling about it being a disgrace and didn't he know who I was. I pulled out three scrunched-up five-pound notes and handed them over.

'Thank you, sir!' he said, doffing his top hat. 'And here are your tickets!' He handed us three pieces of pink card. 'Do have the nicest of evenings.' And with that he turned about and disappeared into the tent.

'Sam?' asked Ho. 'Why did you buy those tickets?'

'Because he was bigger than me.'

'No, no – I mean why did you buy *three* tickets when you already had one in your hand, dumbo?'

Oh, driftwood! I'd forgotten that. I shuffled uncomfortably, but Molly saved me from my embarrassment.

'The boss didn't want to give away the clue!' she said brightly, and tugged Ho's hair.

He kicked her shin in return.

'That's it,' I muttered, shuffling my feet. 'I didn't want to give away the clue! Candy floss, anyone?'

And in we went.

'Twas like being in the stomach of a whale. 'Twas huge, cavernous and smelt slightly of fish. High above, the roof disappeared into darkness and ropes swung and hung from all sides like a well-rigged clipper. Though dry and dusty, Whackett's Circus showed signs of having once been a great circus. Peeling posters and shabby signs hung about like lost pensioners. Somewhere in this place was hidden a clue that would connect Whackett's Circus to Clapshot Towers. But what and how and where and when? The thronging crowd chattered in expectation.

On a podium outside the ring sat a tall woman and a little man. In front of her was a piano and in front of him was a set of drums. Both were beating their instruments as if they had done something very naughty.

Molly and Ho sat clutching their candy floss and looking about excitedly. The music crashed to a conclusion and the lights dimmed. A hush fell over the crowd. Then a single spotlight snapped on and in it stood a familiar figure with a top hat.

'Ladies and gentlemen, welcome to Whackett's Circus! I am Billy Whackett and it gives me the greatest of all pleasures to see you here tonight!'

Tra-laa went the band.

'To open our show I present an act never before seen in this country – a dazzling display of animal skills. Please put your hands together for Octavius the Octopus!'

Into the ring ambled a giant octopus. What a sight it was. A full-sized adult octopus with all eight legs and a slightly sad look in its eyes. The audience gasped in amazement. And then the music started. The octopus began to dance. Well, when I say dance I mean it lumbered back and forth almost in time to the music. 'Twas a strange sight to behold.

Then the music changed and a large hula-hoop was produced. The octopus curled one of its tentacles about the hoop and placed it over its head. Then, with a little difficulty, it began to swing the hoop around its lumpy body. The crowd clapped merrily. Whackett leaped into the ring and addressed the crowd.

'What a talented octopus, ladies and gentlemen! And now the highlight – Octavius the Octopus will raise himself on to the very tips of his tentacles and balance a stick on his head.'

A roll on the drums began. Octavius tried to lift himself, but dropped back down. The audience sighed. He tried once more, but failed. The audience sighed again. Finally, he lifted himself on to the tips of his tentacles and stayed there, looking like an over-inflated ballerina. The audience clapped madly.

Whackett appeared with a stick in his hand. He smiled towards the audience, turned and tossed it in the air. With one swift movement the octopus caught the stick and balanced it on his head. The audience went wild. The octopus bowed politely to the audience and lumbered out of the ring. The applause died down and Whackett stepped into the spotlight.

'May I remind you not to attempt what you've just seen with any octopus you may have at home! But onwards! Bring on the midgets!'

At which point four small people tumbled into the ring. I felt it my duty to keep a note of everything that happened in this case. This is how my notes read later:

1) Funny small people enter.
2) They wear red noses and large shoes.
3) They run about.
4) They pull faces and fall over.
5) One of them sits on a custard pie.
6) A bucket of water is produced.
7) It is poured over the head of one of the small people.
8) They all climb into a big car.
9) It collapses.
10) They all go away again.

At last the band struck up a jolly tune and the midgets took their bows to unenthusiastic applause. Whackett leaped into view and began to introduce the next act, and so the evening wore on. And on. And on.

Finally the last acts took their bows, the musicians took pity on their instruments, and the audience trooped out merrily.

The circus was a mixed bag of brilliance and rot, but it served its purpose and both Molly and Lan Ho were mightily satisfied.

'What was your favourite part?' I asked as we wound our way through the streets of Washed-uponthe- Beach.

'The octopus,' answered Lan Ho, kicking a stone.

'I liked the little people,' said Molly. 'They had such little feet.'

CHAPTER SEVEN

'T was a restless night I spent, tossing and turning in my hammock. 'Twas as if my brain had been nipped by a distant thought. But the next morning my eyes snapped open as the problem I had been tangling with all night plopped into my brain untangled.

'And little feet make little footprints!'

I leapt from my hammock like an eager dolphin and eeled into my clothes. You may snake into yours, but I eel into mine. The sun was a-shining to welcome the day and I, jolly Sam Hawkins, Pirate Detective, was close on the stern of a naughty criminal.

I threw open the door, singing merrily – 'Heave
-ho and up he rises . . .' I straddled the banister of
the staircase and slid downstairs. I jumped off the
banister and bounded into the galley.

All was silent.

I looked about me. 'Twas like the ghost ship
Marie Celeste. Molly and Lan Ho must still be
swinging in their hammocks. Spot shuffled on his
perch, eyeing me sleepily, but I refused to lose
heart.

'Early in the morning!' I sang. 'Morning, Spot!'
I chirped, patting his head.

'Morning, Spot,' he echoed, wincing.

What a beautiful day, I thought, as I set about
making breakfast for my snoring crew. I hadn't felt
this jolly since my first days on the bubbling briny
when I cast all my cares aside, set sail for the
distant horizon and was sick in the captain's hat.

I yanked some pots and pans from the
cupboard and lit the stove.

'What shall we do with a sunken trawler . . . ?'
I sang, chipping something black and green from a
pan.

'Fetch me a potato, Spot,' I ordered. 'Twould be
a breakfast fit for a sea god.

I skipped over to the ship's bell and donged it heartily. Before long, Molly and Lan Ho hoved drowsily into view.

'Yo-ho-ho, it's me motley chums! Moor your weary hulls here a moment,' I sang, drawing back two chairs and dusting down their seats. 'Your jolly boss has made breakfast!' I announced and placed two plates afore them as they sat. " 'Tis your favourite – porridge and chips!'

They looked at me, then at each other, and then, without a word, pounced on this delicacy like desert islanders finding the last coconut.

I watched as the breakfast munched, crunched, slurped and burped into their bellies. The final morsel left their plates and both sat back and sighed.

I sat down beside my crew. 'Now that's safely stowed away, you're probably awondering what makes old Sam so bubbly and buoyant this fine morn.'

Molly and Lan Ho exchanged a glance.

'Not really,' said Molly, scratching her armpit with her breakfast spoon.

I snatched the plates from the table and banged them into the sink.

'Well, I'll tell you anyway. Whilst you two was aslumbering, I was a-tossing and a-turning. I was putting my brain to work on the case in hand. And I have dredged up a clue!'

'Excellent, Sam, well done!' said Ho. Then he smiled. 'But so have we!'

'Oh, yes?' I said, fingering the butter dish. 'And what fascinating clue have you uncovered?'

'Well,' said Molly, 'we were watching those little people doing their tricks last night and I thought, What little feet. And I said to Ho, "What little feet." And then Ho said, "What do little feet make?" And we both said . . .' At this point Ho joined in. '". . . Little footprints!"'

They both smiled.

'We should question the midgets!' Ho concluded.

I flopped into a chair.

'What did you discover, boss?' asked Ho, toying with a chip.

'I've forgotten,' I said, jumping up and clearing the table. 'Tea, anyone?'

Within the hour, Molly and Lan Ho and old Sam Hawkins were standing before Whackett's Circus. I had found the perfect disguise – false moustaches. I handed these out to the crew before knocking on the tent flap.

I heard heavy footsteps approaching and some muttering. A head emerged. It belonged to Whackett.

'Yes?' he snarled.

I waved my library ticket in front of his eyes and put it back in my pocket before he could see it.

'We're from the local authority,' I began loudly.

'And?'

'We've come to inspect your sawdust.'

'Very well. Come in.'

Ha! Fooled him with our disguises.

'Did you enjoy the performance last night?' he asked, leading us towards the ring.

'Well . . . erm . . . yes,' I muttered. 'But today we're here for professional reasons, you understand.'

'I see,' said Whackett, tapping ash from his cigar. 'And do you need to wear a false moustache to do this work?'

I mumbled something about it being a new council rule.

'There's the ring. Don't be all day about it – the midgets are rehearsing in ten minutes,' said Whackett, disappearing around a corner.

We looked about the tent. 'Twas a sad sight without people. The roof hung low and heavy, and the creaky seats looked lost and alone. But this was no time for idle thoughts – we had a case to solve.

I set Molly and Ho the task of inspecting the sawdust, which they took to like ducks to water, measuring pieces of sawdust and weighing clumps of the stuff like experts.

Before long I heard voices approaching and turned to see the four small people entering the ring. These had to be the criminals we sought – no one had smaller feet than they did.

'Good morning,' said one. 'I'm Professor Sebastian Shaw. I believe we are rehearsing this morning.'

'Ha – that is where you are wrong, my sneaky thieves!' And with that I tore the moustache from my face. 'I am Sam Hawkins, Pirate Detective, and I accuse you of stealing the Cut-glass Cutlass from

Washed-upon-the- Beach Museum and selling it to Lady Booming- Clapshot and then stealing it from her as well!'

The midget removed a pipe from his pocket and lit it. His fellow clowns gathered around him.

'Don't be ludicrous,' he said calmly. 'I have no interest in acquiring such an implement. What possible use would that be in my research?'

Molly and Ho removed their disguises and came over to join me. The seven of us stood opposite each other, like battleships ready to fire a broadside. But who would fire first?

'What research?' I asked.

'Well, together with my colleagues here, I am researching the role of the small person in modern society. So far we have discovered that the shorter the person is, the less well respected he is.'

'Shut up, shrimp!' I snapped. 'You stole the cutlass and you have the feet to prove it!'

A second midget stepped forward and introduced himself.

'I am Professor Wallace Wilde and I can only support my colleague's comments. You are accusing the wrong small people.'

Molly stepped forward and picked up Wilde by his elbow.

'That's just what you *would* say. Want a fight?'

Another midget stepped over to Molly and tugged at her kilt.

'I am Professor Oliver O'Casey and I must say I'm intrigued by your response.'

'Why?' said Molly, dropping Wilde.

'What made you say that we *would* say that?'

'What?' 'Well, you spoke as if you knew why we would say something. We are creatures of free will and you, as far as I can ascertain, have no psychic abilities. So, therefore, you cannot possibly know why we say things.'

Molly considered her answer, realized she couldn't think of one and stepped behind Ho.

Another clown stepped forward.

'I am Professor Gilbert Goldsmith and I feel compelled to point out that whatever emotional problems you have, we are not the people to talk to. Have you tried therapy?'

I stamped my foot. 'Don't try wriggling out of this, you tricky sticklebacks. You are villains and that's that!'

I stamped my foot again. Professor Shaw produced a notebook from his pocket and began making notes.

'You, sir, seem to have a lot of pent-up aggression. Perhaps you need to find a way of expressing it. Have you tried boxing?'

'I'm calling the police.' I scrabbled in my pockets. 'Where's my phone? Lan Ho, where've you put my phone?'

Professor Wilde moved over to Shaw.

'Interesting. Notice how he offsets his personal responsibilities on to others.'

Ho produced a mobile phone.

'Call the police afore these villains escape our grasp!' I ordered.

O'Casey joined them.

'Assuming authority without consultation, too. Very interesting.'

Shaw scribbled notes.

Ho was punching buttons on the phone as the midgets peered at me.

'What an intriguing case,' said Shaw. 'I would love to examine your psychological profile a little more closely, but please excuse us – we must practise our juggling.'

The four midgets turned and began arranging their props.

At which point two police officers crashed into the ring – one tall and thin and male, and the other short and fat and female. I had seen them afore – at Clapshot Towers.

'Are you Sam Hawkins, Pirate Detective?' one asked.

'I am, officer, as you well know – and these rapscallions are the thieves who stole the Cut-glass Cutlass!'

'Come along with us then.'

I smiled broadly and pointed at the midgets.

An arm clasped over my hand and forced it behind my back. I heard the click of handcuffs. They were arresting *me*!

'You can't do this!' I bellowed.

'Why is that, sir?'

'Because my feet are too big!

Big feet don't make little footprints!'

But these cries fell on deaf ears as they marched me from the circus ring, crammed me into the police car, clinked me in the slammer and slammed me in the clinker.

And there I would have stayed, were it not for the timely arrival of my old mate Joe 'Greasy' Spoon, the finest solicitor this side of the Old Bailey and an old deckswabbing pal of mine. He'd received a call from Molly and set sail to disentangle me from this muddy muddle.

'We Jack Tars stick together in times of crisis, don't we?' I said as his familiar face entered my cell.

'Indeed we do. I charge £40 an hour plus expenses,' he replied, handing me a list of costs.

'But how are you going to spring me, Joe?' I asked.

'Quite simple, my maritime mate – I'm going to paint your feet!'

He called for Officers Stump and Stibbins, who ambled into the room. They patiently explained to 'Greasy' that I been arrested for breaking and entering Clapshot Towers. Stump produced a photograph of Albert's Memorial. It showed the place covered with footprints, as we had found it. But these were not *my* footprints. These were tiny footprints.

I was incensed.

'How dare you accuse me and my feet! I have the finest feet ever to tread water!'

Joe Spoon quickly soothed the situation with a slick smile.

'Have you measured my client's feet?'

Stump and Stibbins shook their heads.

'Sam Hawkins, remove your shoes and socks!' ordered Joe.

I did so, with the police officers looking on a little bemused as Joe dipped a roller brush in a tin of blue paint and then began painting my feet. I wasn't sure why he was doing it and neither were the police.

'Now,' he said, touching up my big toe, 'step on this piece of paper!' And as I did so, 'Step off again!'

He then produced a tape measure and measured the length of my footprint.

'And what does that say?' he asked Stump.

'Thirty centimetres.'

'Thirty centimetres – exactly!' announced Greasy triumphantly.

'Wait a minute,' interrupted Stibbins. 'Why are we doing this?'

'Proof, officer! Proof of the innocence of my client!'

I tried to pull an innocent face, but it didn't quite work.

Greasy snatched the footprint photo, took his tape measure once more and measured the footprint in the photograph.

'Fifteen centimetres!' Stump and Stibbins nervously said together. 'So he's not guilty.'

'Exactly – because his feet are too big! I thank you!'

Within minutes my shoes were back on my own feet and my feet were on the steps of the police station. I was free, thanks to my old pal 'Greasy' Spoon – but he wasn't a pal for much longer.

What a slimy turncoat he turned out to be. Let me explain. The next day was the trial of those dastardly bad-deed-doers, the Four Midgets. Realizing I was an innocent pirate, Stump and Stibbins had rushed out and arrested them. But who should be sitting in the court defending them? 'Greasy' Spoon himself. I was outraged.

Spoon slithered to his feet and began his defence.

'These are midgets of standing within the community. To accuse them of stealing the famous Cut-glass Cutlass is foolish folly.'

'Foolish folly,' repeated the judge, playing with a yo-yo. This was Justice Bludden 'Guts', once one of the most feared judges in the land. 'Twas he who jailed little Tommy Piper for crab-rustling. 'Twas he who sentenced Lord Balaclava-Fitzbaddley to twenty years' hard labour for whelk-sniffing. Now he was a shrivelled old thing. He looked like a prawn in a cloak.

'Would you like a walnut?' he said to Spoon, proffering a brown paper bag.

'No, thank you, m'lud, all I require is one witness. I call Police Officer Stump.'

Stump nervously adjusted his tie and stepped into the witness box.

Spoon paced before the witness and waved a small pile of papers about his head.

'This is a list from the station computer of all the crimes reported in Washed-upon-the-Beach within the last week. Could you read out the entry for a week last Tuesday.'

Officer Stump stared at the sheet.

'Erm . . .' he began.

'A little louder please.'

'3.30 p.m. – four circus midgets, Shaw, Goldsmith, Wilde and O'Casey, report the theft of four pairs of size thirteen boots from their dressing room.'

Spoon triumphantly snatched the paper from the officer's sweaty palm and held it aloft.

'This entry was made three full days before the first theft of the Cut-glass Cutlass. The shoes that made the footprints at the scenes of the crimes were not in the possession of the midgets when the crimes were committed. I rest my case!'

Justice Bludden 'Guts' giggled and banged his little hammer.

'Case dismissed,' he announced. 'Time for tea!'

'Twas a miscarriage of justice! 'Twas a travesty against all that was shipshape and Bristol fashion! I kicked the chair and steamed towards the exit.

CHAPTER EIGHT

Back at the Naughty Lass I sought solace in a pickled egg.

'Legal poppycock . . .' I muttered between bites, '. . . mumbo-jumbo . . . flim-flam . . .'

Molly sat beside me and stroked the parrot.

'Of course,' she said slowly, 'it was an easy clue to miss.'

'Pah!' I snarled. 'Our first case blown out of the water by that slippery eel of a solicitor. Pah and pah again!'

'Pah again!' echoed the parrot.

I toyed with the clues on the wonky coffee table. What use were they now? However were we to regain our reputation as investigators?

At that moment my mobile phone emitted a jaunty sea-shanty in tinny tones. I punched a button and held it to my ear.

'Hello . . .' I snapped, but heard nothing. 'Hello!'

Not a word came into my shell-like.

'Pah!' I snapped, and tossed the phone across the room.

Ho caught it, dusted it off and was just about to put it in his pocket when he said, 'Wait a minute – it's a text message!'

We huddled around the phone and peered at the tiny window. The message read:

WANT TO SEE REAL TREASURE?

'Yes, we do,' I shouted at the phone.

'Duh! You are so hopeless, Sam! You have to send a message back,' Ho explained.

He deftly tapped in the words I spoke and, a few minutes later, the phone bleeped once more.

THEN BE AT THE PADDLING POOL IN NELSON PARK TONIGHT AT EIGHT.

'Right-o!' I said, and Ho translated my words into taps.

'What's all that about, then?' asked Molly.

'I have no idea,' I said, leaning back in my armchair, 'but it could be our next case.'

The moon was waning as we sat beside the pool, dangling our well-travelled feet in the cooling waters. After the chaos of today the stillness of the water was most welcome. We pondered what our next case would be.

'A lost chimp!' suggested Molly. *Splish, splish.*

'A stolen hat!' said Ho. *Splash, splash.*

'A kidnapping!' said I. *Splosh, splosh.*

Crunch, crunch.

Crunch, crunch?

I thought. Water doesn't crunch.

Molly stopped splishing, Ho stopped splashing and I stopped sploshing.

We looked about in the darkness. Then something moved in the bushes. Ho pointed and gestured. The bush shivered slightly.

And slowly, very slowly, we approached it.

Then, with one massive leap and a huge howl, we jumped on the bush and attempted to grab its occupant. We thrashed about amongst the branches and finally grabbed the stalker.

'It's a squirrel!' said Molly, and began to laugh. When she laughs it sounds like a sink emptying.

Once we realized 'twas nothing but a little furry rodent, we all joined in the laughter.

At that point we heard a roar like twenty sea lions. We turned to see six shadowy figures lurching towards us from out of the bushes. Within seconds they were upon us. I felt my hair being tugged and I fell to the ground. Molly was caught off balance and fell to my side like a washed-up trout. Ho tried kicking our assailants, but to no avail, and he soon joined us on the ground. Just as we were about to try and fight back we found our heads disappearing into three head-sized sacks. Everything disappeared from view and the darkness grew darker still. I felt my hands being tied behind my back and heard a rumbling vehicle approach. We felt ourselves being bundled aboard.

Little did we know that the kidnapping I had hoped for would be our own.

Within half an hour the journey ended and we were marched from the vehicle up a gravelled driveway.

'You can't do this to me!' I protested. 'Don't you know who I am?' In answer to my question I felt the sack being tightened around my neck.

As we crunched forward I tried to make sense of what had happened. Whoever wanted us didn't want us to know where they lived. 'Twere most mysterious goings-on.

I heard a door creak open and realized we were being forced into a building. A sudden shove from behind threw me on to the floor. And then the door creaked closed.

All was silent. Then a voice spoke – a voice I recognized.

'Dis is what happens to dose who mess with me.'

Who was it? I racked my barnacled brain to remember.

'Remove dose masks!'

The sack was suddenly ripped from my head and I blinked. The room was lit with candles and their brightness cut into my eyes. 'Twas a large room and full of riches – every modern technical gadget imaginable and some lovely carpets, too. In the centre was a large golden armchair.

Slowly, very slowly, a familiar face sailed into view. A face like a carved lemon leered down at me and I soon put a name to it.

'Peg-nose Pedro!' I cried.

'Dat's right! Da one and only!'

Peg-nose Pedro, the wickedest and wildest buccaneer in all of Spain.

I gazed at my old adversary – age hadn't withered him. He was still brawny and arrogant. His pencil-thin moustache quivered above slithering lips, which sat on top of his pompous chin. His beady black eyes slunk in the shadows of his fierce eyebrows and scorched their gaze into mine. Out of the centre of his face protruded his famous trademark – a small wooden washing peg where once had been his nose. From the day he sank my toy boat to the day he exploded my dear ship the *Scuttle Butt*, we had been sworn enemies. We fought as boys and we fought as men. And now we had met again.

I looked over at Molly and Ho, who, like me, were seated on the floor, their hands tied behind their backs. I quickly scanned the room. Old Pedro had certainly come a long way since last I laid eyes on him. He'd certainly come into money, too. Lots of it by the looks of things.

'You like my room? I have become a very rich man dince dose days at dea, Dam Hawkins! Today I am the richest man for leagues around.'

He strode back and forth across the huge yellow carpet.

'And how do you make this money?' I asked. 'Stealing from little old ladies?'

'No, no – I dell mobile phones!'

Molly and Ho found it impossible to take their eyes off his peg-nose.

'Dis is what you stare at?' he said, pointing at his polished peg. 'Dis is what I have instead of a dose!'

Molly was the first to speak.

'It's quite nice, actually.'

'Very distinguished,' said Ho politely.

Peg-nose strutted back and forth as he stared down at us.

'I dow what you're dinking!'

He knelt before Ho and Molly.

'You're dinking, who could have done duch a ding? Who could have sliced off my poor defenceless dose? What vile and violent varlet would do dis ding?'

'Who?' asked Molly and Ho together.

'Dat man!' he bellowed, and pointed at me.

Ho and Molly turned in disbelief to their leader.

'It was an accident!' I pleaded. 'It was very dark in the butcher's shop. I was young. I was trying to impress my boss. I was chopping off all sorts of things!'

He strutted over to me. His eyes glared and I quaked below him.

'Imagine what smells I've missed! Oh, to sniff one flower. To idhale the aroma of fried bacon. But dever shall I smell dem again. Danks to you!'

'I'm sorry, I'm sorry, I'm sorry!' I tried to muster some dignity before my crew. 'But what do you want? Why have you brought us here?'

Peg-nose brought his lemon face level with mine and stared at me.

'I have brought you here to avenge my dose!'

With that he clapped his hands and the ruffians who'd kidnapped us manhandled us into three small chairs, whilst Peg-nose strutted over to the large golden chair that dominated the room.

'And how shall I avenge my dose, you're probably dinking.'

He clapped his hands once more.

'Bring forth my bounty!'

The doors slid open and in walked another ruffian, carefully carrying before him a long, red-velvet box, which he gently placed on a low table in the centre of the room. He stepped back and bowed.

Peg-nose leapt from his chair to the box.

'In here is treasure! Treasure the like of which you have dever deen! My treasure.'

He threw open the lid of the box.

We leaned as far forward as our ropes would allow. And there, nestling in the comfortable padding of the box, was none other than the Cut-glass Cutlass! 'Twas a stirring sight. 'Twas even more beautiful than I remembered. This was the first time I had seen it since my childhood. The sparkle of the candlelight danced across the hilt and winked at us.

But how had it come into the hands of Peg-nose Pedro?

'You stole it!' I exclaimed. 'Doh, I didn't deal it!' snapped Peg-nose, slamming the lid. 'I bought it.

I'm a very rich man. I dell mobile phones. I bought it from a well-respected dource.'

'A well-respected horse?' asked Molly.

'Doh, doh, doh! Dource – as in ketchup.'

'He means a well-respected *source*!' I explained.

'But why are you showing it to us?' asked Molly.

'Good question,' said Peg-nose.

'Thank you,' I said.

Peg-nose began pacing back and forth.

'I know the cutladd has been stolen afore. And whodoever id stealing it will make an attempt to steal it once more. And I don't want dat to happen.'

I shuffled in my ropes.

'So?'

'Do, my little dose-sticker, dat is where you come in. You and your friends are to guard it.'

'Oh, is that all?'

'Doh, dat is not all!' he cried, then recovered his composure. 'I have readon to believe there may be an attempt to steal it todight. If the cutladd is dot stolen I keep it and I'll be happy. If the cutladd *id* stolen I dimply slice off your dose and I'll be even happier!'

'Slice off my nose?' I whimpered.

'From dostril to dostril!'

Ho suddenly spoke up.

'How can we guard the cutlass with our hands tied behind our backs?'

Pedro paused and scratched his peg.

'I was just going to mention dat. Untie dem!' he ordered a thug.

The thug obeyed his boss and we sat rubbing our wrists.

Pedro surveyed the scene, sniffed (well, tried to) and strutted from the room. His thugs followed behind, slamming the door as they went. A key rattled in the lock and the room fell silent.

Molly and Ho looked at me with utter disdain. 'Oh, brilliant!' said Ho. 'It's at times like this I wonder about all the other people who could have rescued me from Kowloon Bay. Hundreds must have walked past. Millionaires, kings, queens. I could be sitting in a palace now, Sam Hawkins, sipping willow tea and playing Peking poker. But, oh no, *you* had to go and rescue me, didn't you? And look where I've ended up.'

I stared back, unable to offer support.

Molly and Ho shuffled to the other side of the room and mumbled under their breath. I pondered our problem. Then an idea plopped into my brain. Suppose, as Peg-nose suggested, someone attempted to steal the cutlass tonight? Suppose we captured the skull-dugging bad-deed-doer? We could finally find out who was behind the thefts! That would mean I could solve the case of the Cut-glass Cutlass *and* make amends to Peg-nose Pedro. Land two pilchards with one net, as it were. I explained the plan to the crew.

We all swore we wouldn't sleep a wink that night.

CHAPTER NINE

H a! – Peg-nose Pedro thought he'd caught us good and proper. Ha! But that's where he was wrong. All we needed to do was stay awake and alert and we'd reel in the real villain and make peace with Pedro all in one go. Now, I'd taken many a night-watch and often stood alone atop a tall mast in a freezing crow's-nest with only a flask of piping gruel to keep me company, but 'twas the other pair I was worried about.

As I pondered these thoughts, Ho made a discovery that would help us through the night.

'Oh, wow!' he said, tugging a small box from behind a chair. 'Oceanopoly!' It seemed Peg-nose had left an odd assortment of games to amuse us through the night, and Oceanopoly was one of 'em. 'Tis known throughout the seafaring world and has kept many a dull voyage alive with joy and frolics. A single game could last for hours and hours. Perfect.

Ho tore off the lid. Molly lifted out the board, unfolded it and placed it on the floor. We all knew the rules.

'I want to be the cannon!' exclaimed Molly, snatching up the little silver cannon before any of us could disagree.

'I'll be the porthole, then!' said Ho, grabbing a counter of a similar size.

This left me with the choice of the rudder or the anchor. I chose the anchor.

Now, as I said, Oceanopoly is a long game – legend tells of two sailors stranded on a iceberg who made a game last three months. At sea, with only the odd porpoise for company, it can seem fascinating and delightful. But we were not at sea and the game, to be blunt as a cuttlefish, was as dull as dish water.

We began. I was soon in the lead. I'd played the game many times afore and knew all the backwaters and tricks. I soon owned Portsmouth,

Plymouth, the English Channel and the Straits of Gibraltar. I placed two taverns on Portsmouth and had already collected 200 gold coins in rent. This was enough to sustain my interest, but Molly and Ho hadn't my concentration and soon began to wilt.

Molly was the first to go. She was sitting by the board staring at a Treasure Chest card when a large yawn erupted from her face. She sounded like a distressed whale. Her eyelids hesitated but finally fell, she keeled over and slumped into a snoring mound.

Ho watched her go and shrugged as he picked up the dice and threw them across the board. The candle spluttered behind him as he yawned and hopped his porthole seven spaces, landing on the 'Go Straight to the Brig' square.

I threw the dice and landed on the Treasure Chest. I grabbed a card. "'Congratulations, it is your berth day. Collect twenty gold coins from each player." Pay up, Ho! Ho?'

I looked up. Where was he? I put my palm to my shell-like and detected a faint snoring. I looked under the table. There lay Ho, curled up like an eel, with his head on Molly's feet.

Pah – let them sleep! I'd weathered worse storms than this. When you're clinging to the rigging in high winds, sewing up a ghastly gash made by enemy gunfire, there's no time for forty winks. When you're looking out for icebergs in the chilling waters of the North Atlantic, there's no time for snoring. At least I knew *I'd* be able to stay awake throughout the night!

☠   ☠

I awoke the next morning to find a seagull pecking at my head. How the briny did a seagull get into the room? The door had been locked. I rubbed my sleepy eyes and looked about. Molly and Ho lay to my starboard side, nestling on the floor like two beached seals. And there behind them was the answer to my question.

A window high up in the wall had been broken. That was how the seagull got in. I flapped my arms and squawked like a hawk. The seagull yelped, flopped towards the broken window and flew out into the crisp morning air.

Sunlight streamed through the window and I stood up. I ambled over to Molly and Ho and gave them both a playful kick to awaken them. They mumbled, yawning and stretching.

'Morning, Sam! What are you making for breakfast?'

'And what exactly could we have for breakfast, Ho?'

'We could have red herrings,' said Molly, waving one in the air.

'Where did you get that?' I snapped, snatching the fish and peering at it.

'There's a load of them under the window,' Molly pointed out.

I stomped over and, sure enough, the floor was strewn with little red herrings.

'Barnacles!' I cursed.

'Sam, Sam, Sam!'said Ho, tugging at my sleeve.

'What?' I bellowed.

I turned to see Ho pointing towards the ground and quaking slightly.

'Little footprints!' he hissed.

He was right – the floor was covered in the selfsame muddy footprints we had seen afore.

Then, in unison, two words splashed from all our mouths.

'*The cutlass*!'

We ran over to the table. The box was shut. My salty fingers tapped on the lid. I gulped a dry gulp and, with my last ounce of courage, I tore it open.

The box was empty!

I slammed the lid shut.

'A trick of the light!' I cried. 'Or maybe we're still asleep!'

I opened the lid again.

The box was still empty.

'Oh, my breeches and trinkets,' I mumbled.

Molly placed a consoling arm about my shoulders. 'You're going to have your nose sliced off, boss.'

At that point a key rattled in the door.

I clutched the box to my beating heart as we stood in Peg-nose's office. I looked about as I waited for him to finish his phone call. The room was not my idea of good taste. I mean, what use is a desk made of solid gold? I got a waft of his aftershave – Canal No. 9. Very posh stuff. I noticed the grotty stench coming from my own armpit and sighed.

Peg-nose stabbed a button on his mobile phone and shot an order to one of his assistants.

'Prepare a consignment of 200 Hornblower 1805s for Mobile Home in the High Street. The ones with the flashy aerials.'

A hairy cohort gave a hearty salute and left the room. Peg-nose scribbled a short note on his hand to remind himself of the order, then turned to us.

He rubbed his peg thoughtfully and regarded us with inky eyes. His bejewelled fingers glinted as he ran them through his oil-slick hair. A deep and deadly soul lurked at the heart of this man. Even at school he would slink in the shadows in the playground. He would pull children's ears and run away. He once gutted my pet halibut and sold it to the local fishmonger.

'Sleep well, did we?' he enquired with a slithering smile.

'Very well, thank 'ee,' I said, doffing my hat.

'Like a ship's log,' added Ho.

'We weren't disturbed once,' said Molly. 'Honest.'

Peg-nose grabbed a roll of parchment from the table and began idly snipping off pieces with a long pair of scissors.

'Dothing disturbed you?' he asked, and snipped some more.

We shook our heads vigorously. He was taunting me. I knew it. Just like he used to at school.

'Dothing at all?'

We shook our heads even more vigorously.

'Dot even de loud sound of breaking glass at middight?' he shouted, screwing up the paper and throwing it at us.

'No, no, no, no!' we said, sounding like startled penguins.

Peg-nose slid from behind the desk and came over to us.

'*I* was woken in de dight by de dound of breaking glass! But I did not worry because I dew my treasure was in dafe hands!'

Molly and Ho looked at their safe hands nervously.

'Do you're daying the Cut-glass Cutlass has dot been dolen? So I don't get to 'lice off your dose?'

I covered my nose, slightly losing my grip on the box. Peg-nose placed his hand on it

'Or even kill you?'

His hand stayed there a moment. Could he feel my heart beating at a rare rate of knots? Could he see a tiny trickle of sweat winding its way down my cheek? He tugged at the box and I reluctantly released it.

He took the box to his desk, gently placed it there and then turned his back on us.

'So your fate is dealed in dis box. When I open dis lid I'll doh whether I still own the most priceless cutlass in dautical history or whether to chop off your dose.'

He leaned forward and slowly, very slowly, opened the lid.

The box, as you know, was empty. Empty apart from Ho's penknife, which didn't fool him for a minute.

'Dolen!' he bellowed, and whirled around.

I wish I could tell you what his face looked like, but I can't – we weren't there! We had slipped through his fingers like well-oiled pilchards.

We shot through the corridors like a school of tuna, twisting and turning at every corner. Twice we were set upon by ruffians, and twice we wormed and kicked our way out of their grasp. In the distance, Peg-nose Pedro barked orders back and forth.

We burst out of Peg-nose's home, pausing for a moment on the gravel driveway with one question quivering on our lips:

How were we to escape?

Ho's elbow was in my ear, but I didn't complain. In fact, I couldn't complain, because Molly's foot was in my mouth.

By clever cunning we had managed to hide away in the very consignment of mobile phones Peg-nose was sending to town. We had climbed aboard a deserted delivery van and sealed ourselves in a large cardboard box.

The delivery van bumped and banged along the road to Washed-upon-the-Beach. But I didn't care about the discomfort. We were free. I felt my nose and breathed a sigh of relief.

After a while the van screeched to a halt and we heard the door creak open. Mumbled voices exchanged pleasantries and we felt ourselves being dragged off the van. We heard the creaky doors slam and the sound of the van speeding away.

We felt the box being dragged into the shop and then all fell silent.

Ho mumbled something.

'Take Molly's ear out of your mouth!' I instructed him.

'What do we do now, O great and clever leader?' asked Ho sarcastically.

I pressed my eye to the hand-hole in the box and stared out. My eye darted back and forth, assessing the situation.

'We're in the stockroom. Abandon box!' I poked my hand through the hole and was just about to start peeling away the tape which sealed the box when I had the fright of my nautical life. Every single mobile phone in the box suddenly burst into life. Jingles and classics and theme tunes all splashed and crashed together in a whirlpool of unharmonic noise. 'Twas an ear-shattering cacophony of sounds.

I grabbed one phone, stabbed a button and held it to my ear. The others fell silent.

'Hello?'

On the other end I heard a familiar voice.

'I dew that was how you escaped!'

'Twas Peg-nose Pedro! He'd figured out our plan. But we were still far from his clutches.

'Then why don't you come and find us?' I taunted him, and stuck out my tongue for good measure.

'I shall find you, Dam Hawkins,' Peg-nose growled. 'I shall avenge my dose. And when I do I shall tie you to a chair and 'lice off your . . . *Please top up your credit, please top up your credit, please top up your credit, please top up your credit . . .*'

I dropped the mobile phone, leaving the computerized female voice chattering away on the floor. I hacked away at the tape and we soon extracted ourselves from the box.

There, standing in the stockroom, was a tall man in a grey suit. On his chest was a badge that read 'Mobile Home General Manager', and on his face was an expression that read 'Anger'!

'What are you doing in my stockroom?' he demanded, and tried to grab me.

Like a conga eel I slipped to one side and made for the door. Molly and Ho split up and darted past him on either side. He didn't know which to grab first and missed both of them.

We sped through the gadget shop, knocking over displays as we ran. I tried gabbling an apology as we hared towards the exit, but it fell on deaf ears. We sped out of the shopping centre and set a course for the Naughty Lass.

☠ ☠

That evening, before a roaring fire, we recounted the tale of our day's escapades to Spot.

'It all went like a dream!' I announced modestly.

At this point, Ho's face changed. He suddenly looked confused.

'I had a dream last night, Sam. At least, I think it was a dream.' He sipped his night-time grog and tried to recall it.

'I was asleep with my head on Moll's foot. And something – something slimy – slid across my thigh. I awoke to see it go past my face.' He fell silent and slurped some more grog.

'But what was it you saw, my hearty haddock?' I asked, leaning closer.

He said something in Chinese and wiggled his arm in the air.

'I don't know the English word, Sam.'

Molly jumped over to the bookshelves and tugged out a dusty Chinese–English dictionary. She handed it to Ho, who anxiously flicked through the pages.

Suddenly he stopped and pointed a quivering finger at a word.

When I saw what it was my heart turned cold.

The word was: '*Tentacle!*'

CHAPTER TEN

B*ang, bang, bang!*
I muttered and turned over in my hammock.

Bang, bang, bang!

What blithering, blinking, barmy boatswain was amaking that racket?

Pah! I clambered from the hammock muttering nautical curses. I looked towards the bedside clock, which told me I'd been disturbed from my precious slumber at three o'clock in the morning. Three o'clock! The mucky buccaneer better have a good reason for it. I wrapped the duvet like a toga about my hull and padded downstairs.

The letter box flapped wildly with each bang of the door. Silhouetted through the window I saw a figure wearing a top hat.

I cautiously flipped open the letter box and peered out. An angry face peered back. 'Twas the face of Whackett of Whackett's Circus. What did the fellow want?

I slid back all the bolts, unlocked all the locks and carefully opened the door.

Whackett slammed the door out of my hand and crashed it against the wall. He exploded into the hall and grabbed me by the duvet. He brought his pointy nose up against mine and I could smell whisky on his greased moustache.

'Where are my midgets?' he bellowed.

'Twas a strange question to be asked at such an early hour, but I had my naval senses about me and quick as a flash I replied,' . . . erm . . .'

He released me and shot anxious looks about the hall.

'If I find you're harbouring my midgets, I'll give you what for!'

'What for?' I asked.

'Precisely!' he said, and stomped into the living room.

Before I could stop him, Whackett was rummaging through every cupboard and drawer in the room. Books and charts flew through the air. 'Twas like being at sea in the mightiest of storms, but the centre of this storm was Whackett.

Spot's cage was tossed aside, with poor Spot cowering behind his little mirror in fright. But no midgets appeared.

'I don't have your midgets!' I pleaded. 'Put down that bucket!'

Whackett was not listening and strode off. He snarled and barked and chopped his way through the undergrowth of the kitchen.

'They were found not guilty of stealing that cutlass, released from court and I haven't seen them since!'

'I know they were and neither have I! Please put that mop back!'

Ignoring my protests he clonked upstairs into Molly's bedroom. There was an astonished scream and Whackett staggered out, looking flushed.

He tried Ho's room, which was empty, then thundered into the bathroom, where he found Ho asleep in the bath. He looked about, getting more and more frustrated.

'Midgies, midgies, midgies, where are you?'

He tried the attic and the cellar, but soon he had to admit I was telling the truth.

'There are no midgets here!' he said, sitting on the stairs, tapping his whip against the banister and thinking. I hitched up my duvet indignantly.

'Just what I said.'

Whackett fingered his moustache and a sadness fell over him.

'My prize midgets have gone astray. However shall I survive without them?' He started to sniff slightly.

I sat beside him and put a comforting arm about his shoulder.

'Fret not, Whackett, I'm sure you'll work something out.'

Whackett leapt to his feet and suddenly snarled, 'Indeed I shall. You will be their replacements! Be at the circus at nine o'clock to begin rehearsals.'

He stomped down the stairs and headed for the door.

'But we couldn't possibly . . .'

He paused in the doorway and turned.

'However, if you refuse my very kind offer, I shall have no alternative but to report to the police how I was visited by three people pretending to be from the local authority . . .'

I obviously looked confused.

'Sawdust inspectors!' he spat, and slammed the door shut. A stuffed salmon tottered and fell from the wall.

Oh, blowholes!

☠   ☠

I revealed the news to Ho and Molly at breakfast, bracing myself for a tidal wave of complaints.

'Brilliant!' Molly cried, and did a little dance. 'We're going to join the circus!'

Ho, however, wasn't happy.

'If I'd wanted to join the circus, I'd have been rescued from Kowloon Bay by a trained gorilla,' he said, and stared at me.

'You could do a Chinese firework display!' I said, then looked up at the singed ceiling and shuddered. Ho followed my gaze.

'Hmm, now that could be fun!' he said, cheering up.

Well, the crew were happy, but what was *I* to do? I thought about the skills I could bring to a circus act – I could box a compass, I could splice a mainbrace, I could pickle a herring, I could run up the Jolly Roger. Which should it be?

We reluctantly made our way towards the circus. Molly and Ho trotted on ahead, I trailed behind. I couldn't juggle, I couldn't walk a tightrope. I wasn't going to learn anything new at my age. As the saying goes, you can't teach an old sea dog new tricks.

☠   ☠

In the dressing-room mirror I stared at the white face that stared back. Had I really come to this? Sam Hawkins, who once shared a crow's-nest with the most grizzled pirates in the Med, who once rescued Princess Nelly from the evil clutches of Monteray George, who could handle a rapier as well as any privateer at sea . . . Sam Hawkins reduced to a circus clown. Could it get any worse?

'And here's your custard pie!' said Whackett. 'Follow me!'

I put on my clown shoes and followed him. I walked like a penguin and felt like a fool.

Back in the circus ring, Ho was scuttling about with arms full of fireworks, helped by Molly. Whackett was obviously unsure about this but was prepared to give it a go.

'Now, Hawkins! Let me teach you how to throw a custard pie. First, you place the pie in the centre of your palm . . . Stop playing that harmonica whilst I'm teaching!' he bellowed at the octopus, who had just mastered a tune.

Ho was tugging at Whackett's sleeve.

The ringmaster looked down at Ho's eager face and lowered his pie.

'Yes?'

'Matches! I need matches, Billy!'

'Go and look in my office. And don't call me Billy.'

Ho scurried away.

'Now,' said Whackett, returning to the lesson. 'Notice how my arm is bent here and my legs are slightly apart, giving me a little spring. I take aim and throw . . .' He released the pie. I watched fly it through the air . . . and land on my face with a loud splosh.

Sam Hawkins, who rescued thirteen gerbils from the burning remains of the Black Spot Tavern . . .

I wiped the custard from my chin.

'Very impressive!' I said, unimpressed.

'And also very funny. Now you try!'

I clutched another pie, bent my arm as instructed, parted my legs, took aim and released the pie.

The pie hit Whackett full in the face. But I didn't hear a splosh. No, what I heard was this:

BOOM!!

'Twas like 100 cannons fired at once and it came from Whackett's office – as did a great deal of smoke.

I ran towards the office door, followed by Molly.

Whackett pulled out a mobile phone and called the fire brigade.

I wafted the smoke about. 'Ho!' I called. 'Ho, where are you?'

From the smoke emerged a black-faced Ho, his clothes in scorched tatters.

'I found the matches!' he said brightly.

The smoke was slowly starting to disperse, revealing the remains of Whackett's office. Burnt papers lay everywhere. I peered into the smoky room and my beady eye fell upon a fascinating sight. At the far end was a safe, its door swinging limply open. I rubbed my eyes – was it smoke or disbelief? For there inside the safe were four small pairs of boots. Tiny boots.

My thoughts were cut short as Whackett thundered over, pushed me aside and slammed shut the office door.

At that point a large man stumbled across the circus ring, grasping a trailing yellow hose and sweating slightly. He was wearing a fireman's uniform at least two sizes too small and a helmet at least two sizes too big. He was followed by another eager man wearing a uniform two sizes too big and a helmet two sizes too small.

'Where's the fire?' they panted, swapping helmets.

I pointed towards the office. The large fireman charged the door, shattering it open, and launched a jet of cold water into Whackett's office. The other fireman quickly followed him in with extinguishers and sprayed the entire office with white foam. Whackett watched, aghast.

Before long the firemen had finished and the last drops of foam and water plopped from their pipes. The office swam with water.

The sweaty fireman pulled a form from his pocket and asked Whackett to fill it in. In a daze Whackett did so.

'Oh, so you're Whackett?' the fireman said, looking at the form. 'You must be very proud of your midgets! Huge stars, eh?'

'What?' Whackett stared at him.

'Look . . .'

The fireman pulled a magazine from his pocket and shoved it under Whackett's nose.

Local Midgets Become Singing Stars
Four local midgets, who recently appeared at Whackett's Circus, have been snapped up by a London pop music promoter and turned into the latest boy band sensation – Slinky!

Whackett snatched the paper and stared at it. He scrunched it up and looked like he'd swallowed an onion.

'What am I going to do?'

The fireman scratched his armpit and thought. Suddenly his face lit up.

'You should form a tribute band!'

'A what?' snarled Whackett.

'You know, a group that looks like a famous band, sounds like a favourite band, plays the music of a famous band, but isn't, in fact, famous!'

'And is half the price!' Whackett said slowly. He patted the fireman on the back, turned on his heel and hurried into his smouldering office. He tore open a scorched drawer and pulled out a charred address book, then he delicately flipped open a page and tapped a number into his slightly melted phone.

'Barrie, it's Whackett – I need four midgets by two o'clock today! And they must be able to sing.' He turned to Molly, Ho and me. 'You can go now. You're fired!' He turned his back on us.

The firemen curled up their hose. I wiped the make-up from my face and pulled off the red clown's nose. As we left the circus we heard the wailing sound of a harmonica in the distance.

CHAPTER ELEVEN

Next day I sat upstairs in my bedroom in my squeaky, creaky rocking chair, pumped a seashanty out of my dusty squeeze-box and considered the case. I needed to organize my salty brain. I set aside my squeeze-box, pulled a parchment from my tunic and began scribbling.

Sam Hawkins's Case Notes
The Case of the Cut-glass Cutlass
Three thefts:
1) From the museum
2) From Clapshot Towers
3) From Peg-nose Pedro
What have all these got in common?

Four clues:
  1) Lots of tiny footprints
  2) Photocopy of an unknown bottom
     (with scribbled note about the wreck
     of the BENBO)
  3) Red herrings (numerous)
  4) A tentacle (one sighting)
Suspects:
  Nil.

I scratched my head with the pen and considered the first part. Lady Booming-Clapshot, Mayor Lola Schwartz and Peg-nose Pedro had all wanted the cutlass. All three had the money to buy the cutlass. All three had been sold the cutlass. But who was doing the selling? Who was doing the stealing? Was it the same person? Who was devious enough to pull off such a scam? The sighting of the tentacle, I decided, was just a fuzzy figment of Ho's over-excited imagination. I tapped my nose with the pen, lost in thought. Stump and Stibbins of the Washed-upon-the-Beach police had drawn a blank on all these clues. Ha, this was a job for a professional. Sam Hawkins was not going to give in.

I leaped from my chair, the sheaf of notes in my hand, and made for the stairs.

As I creaked my way down I suddenly stopped. My shell-like ear was hearing giggling. Not only giggling but bubbling. What was all this, I wondered, as I approached the kitchen door and stepped in.

There in the centre of the room were Molly and Ho, gathered around a thick book at the breakfast table. Molly was giggling and pointing. Bubbling behind them was a blackened pan on the hob.

'What's this, my budding bookworms?'

Molly and Ho looked up and smiled.

'Accounts!' explained Ho.

Bubble, bubble went the contents of the pan.

'Accounts of what – of derring-do on the high seas?' I asked, swishing my pen through the air like a sword.

'No, Sam, these are business accounts – from Whackett's Circus!'

Bubble, bubble. It smelt like a well-rotted carpet. Must be dinner, I thought.

'When the office exploded I was having a sneaky look around. I didn't see anything suspicious. Then, underneath a filing cabinet, I found this. It will tell us if Whackett has been up to no good!'

'Whackett, of course!' I announced. 'He's pulling off a scam. 'Twas Whackett who stole the cutlass from the museum. He sold it to Lady Booming-Clapshot and, here's the clever part, then he stole it back again! Do you see? *Then* he sold it to Peg-nose Pedro and, wait for it, stole it back again! And now he's probably going to sell it to someone else! Well done!'

I slapped my oriental sidekick on the back.

'If Whackett has been receiving any mysterious payments,' I went on, 'it'll be in his accounts book. In here is the evidence that will convict Whackett and prove him to be the vicious shark that he really is. I'll bet my breeches on it!'

Ho and Molly looked at me as the pan bubbled away.

Then they looked at my breeches.

Then we opened the accounts book.

Two hours later I was standing in the kitchen in my underpants.

'You must have missed something!' I hissed as Molly pinned my breeches to the notice board like a trophy.

'No!' said Ho, rubbing his eyes wearily. 'We didn't find anything. There's nothing there, Sam Hawkins . . .' He pulled a face. 'Pirate Detective.'

'Oh, winkles!' I cursed.

Suddenly the bubbling stopped.

We looked about.

'Oh, no!' said Ho. 'I forgot to turn down the . . .'

KER-SPLOSH! Dribble, dribble.

With one gurgling sneeze the entire contents of the bubbling pan exploded. The sprout soup (a favourite of Ho's) sloshed over the accounts book. Molly shrieked with surprise and dropped her lemonade. It, too, landed on the book.

I couldn't believe my eyes as the disgusting cocktail spread over the book like an oil slick.

'You've ruined the evidence!' I cried. Ho grabbed a tea towel and immediately began mopping up the lemonade and sprout soup. He wiped the book down, which was a mistake. The accounts were written in ink and with each wipe Ho was obliterating the writing.

Before I could stop him there was nothing left to read. Just a swirling mass of messy ink.

A heavy silence filled the room, broken by the occasional squelch of Ho's tea towel.

They both looked at me, expecting an eruption of rude words, but suddenly my thoughts were elsewhere.

I was looking down at the book. Slowly, very slowly, something was happening.

The others gathered about their captain and we watched in amazement as a whole new set of numbers started to appear in the book.

I peered closely. What was happening?

Ho had the answer.

'Invisible ink!' he cried. 'The lemonade and sprout soup have chemically reacted with the invisible ink and are making it visible again.'

'So there *is* evidence in this accounts book!' I gasped.

And this is what we read:

£4,000 payment received 5th August
£4,000 payment received 14th August
£4,000 payment received 21st August

'Molly,' I said proudly.

'Yes, boss?'

'Take my breeches off the wall, would you?'

I sat on my squeaky, creaky rocking chair pumping a tune from my squeeze-box and mused on the new evidence. Whackett had been receiving huge payments. He wanted to hide these payments. Why? Maybe the payments were, as I thought, for the Cut-glass Cutlass. But how could we prove it? And how was he stealing the cutlass each time? So many questions to be answered. 'Twas time to address my crew once more. I went downstairs.

'Crew meeting!' I announced, donging the ship's bell on the mantelpiece.

Ho, Molly and Spot gathered around.

'Now then, my hearty shoal of catfish. 'Tis time to make our next move. Slowly but surely, we're making good headway and our slippery criminal is in our sights. Whackett has been receiving payments. He wishes to keep these payments secret. I have been musing on our next move and have reached a conclusion. We have only one course of action, only one direction in which we must sail!'

The crew leaned forward, eager to hear my every word. They were a good and noble crew who'd follow me through thick and thin – well-trained mariners who'd do precisely as their captain ordered.

'To find the clues to guide us to our final destination, we're going to rejoin the circus!'

Molly looked at Spot. Spot looked at Ho. Ho looked at Molly and they all looked at me.

'No, we're not!' they said together.

'Mutiny!' I bellowed. 'I'll make you walk the plank . . . I'll keel-haul you . . . I'll have you flogged from dusk to dawn . . .' I thought for a moment. 'You can have free ice cream!'

They nodded their approval. Later I sat at my desk with my case notes before me and wrote:

The Case of the Cut-glass Cutlass
Suspects: one – Whackett of Whackett's Circus

CHAPTER TWELVE

'Side, together, side, kick!'

What a mighty odd world was the world of show business! I'd seen many bizarre sights in my years on the bubbling briny, but none as strange as four small people in silver suits being taught to dance by a circus ringmaster.

'No, kick with the left leg, Bingo!'

The tiny people were not over-burdened with talent and poor old Whackett had his work cut out to train them. The previous four midgets were sailing high in the pop charts with a song called 'The Bobby Shaftoe Mega Mix' and he was determined to copy them. There was lots of money to be made in the pop world and Whackett wanted some of it.

'No, somersault, Bingo! Smartie, put down that custard pie!'

Molly, Ho and I drifted quietly into the front seats and watched the master showman at work.

'Right, side, together, side, kick!'

Whackett was an interesting fish – a talented showman – but below the surface ran cruel waters.

'If you do that again, Bingo, I'll use my stick!'

During a break in rehearsals I moved over to him.

'Mr Whackett . . .'

'Oh, juggling balls! This is all I need. Come to inspect my sawdust again, have you?'

He poured himself a paper cup full of water and drank.

'No, no,' I said, doffing my hat. ''Tis another mission I'm here on, sir.'

Whackett eyed me suspiciously.

'Go on!'

'We was a-wondering, sir, if, perhaps, you maybe would, possibly, consider . . .' I gulped '. . . letting us rejoin the circus.'

Whackett laughed a cackling laugh that made a nearby seal look up in surprise.

'You? After what you did?'

'Erm . . . yes, sir, we're a little short of cash at the moment and . . .'

He was about to throw away the paper cup but suddenly paused.

'And what possible talent do you have to offer, pray tell?'

At this point an arrow shot through Whackett's cup.

☠   ☠

Luckily, Ho had some bandages.

'This is my pointing finger!' moaned Whackett as Ho tended to him. 'I need it. I introduce the acts with this finger!' He snatched his hand from Ho and tried a few gestures. 'No, it doesn't point nearly so well with a bandage on it.'

We were in Whackett's new office, which had been hastily constructed near the old one. 'Twas not an easy place to get to. We had to climb rope ladders and everything.

Molly stood to one side, twanging her bow sheepishly. Whackett looked over to her.

'Despite my injury, I have to say you are very good with a bow and arrow. I might be able to use you in the circus.' Molly's eyes lit up. 'What you need is someone to be a target – not me, my limbs are far too valuable, but someone who wouldn't mind having an apple shot from his head.'

For reasons I shall never fathom they all turned to look at me. Even the parrot.

'No, no, not me.' 'Why not?'

'Dry land, you see! It's a problem. After all those years at sea, you see, I can't stop bobbing up and down!'

I bobbed up and down to demonstrate.

'Perfect!' announced Whackett. 'A moving target!'

There was a knock at the door. Whackett jumped to his feet and answered it. There sat the squat and sad figure of the octopus. He stared at us with oil-black eyes. In his mouth he held a rolled-up newspaper. He must have clambered from the ring and up the rope ladder. What an athletic octopus! I was dragged from my thoughts as Whackett snatched the newspaper from its mouth and slammed the door.

'How did that octopus get all the way up here?' I asked.

'It's all part of the new act – I've been teaching it to climb. Right, we'll rehearse later – off you go!'

And with that he turned his attention to the *Ringmasters' Gazette*.

☠   ☠

I stood all alone in the centre of the massive circus ring, tied to a tent pole the size of an oak tree. Molly approached me and placed an apple on my head. I smiled nervously. Well, when I say nervously, I mean I was terrified. My teeth were chattering in their dock and my sea legs were banging together like Japanese fighting fish. Now, I trusted Molly – we'd sailed through many a storm together and always pulled into harbour safe and sound – but I'd seen her shoot arrows afore. I still have the scars.

She winked at me in a reassuring way, which only made me feel worse, and walked off. About five yards away she turned and drew her bow.

'I'm over here!' I shouted to attract her attention.

She took aim and, without hesitating, released an arrow. Whackett watched as it flew through the air, but his expression changed as he realized the arrow wasn't heading for my head, but *his* head. He grimaced. At which point Spot flapped from out of nowhere, calmly snatched the arrow from the air, changed its direction and stabbed it into the apple on my head.

Whackett leapt to his feet, applauding wildly.

'Where did the parrot learn that?' he exclaimed, patting me heartily on the back.

'Oh, it was just a-something we used to do to occupy the long hours on desert islands,' I gulped, and managed to stagger away.

A sad tune was drifting from Whackett's office. 'Twas being played on the harmonica. I looked up and saw the old octopus gazing down at me through the window. As he caught my gaze he stopped suddenly and disappeared from view. When he reappeared he was waving a copy of the Washed-upon-the Beach *A to Z*. Hmmm, I thought, Why the Washed-upon-the-Beach road map?

'I'm looking for a volunteer!' said a female voice I'd not heard before. I dragged myself from my musings and turned towards it.

'I'm Maude,' she said.

She was a rusty old tug. She wore a blonde wig from underneath which poked snow-white hair. Her face was almost orange with make-up and her lips looked like two chilli peppers. She flapped her spidery eyelashes at me and spoke again.

'I'm Maude,' she repeated.

'Then you should untie your ropes!' I hooted. 'Moored! Get it?' I nudged Ho in the ribs.

'I'm looking for a volunteer!' she said, clearly not understanding my very witty joke. She walked towards me with her hand outstretched. As she approached I grabbed Ho's hand and placed it in hers.

'What are you doing? Get off!' He struggled, but Maude was a tough old fish and tugged him towards the centre of the ring.

She clapped her hands. A pack of grunting stagehands trundled in something huge, 'bout the size of an average frigate. But what it was I couldn't tell, for 'twas hidden beneath yards of grey canvas.

'I don't want to do this. What have you got me into, Sam Hawkins?' Ho hissed nervously.

Maude silenced him with a polite slap.

'Now, ladies and gentleman, this kind young man has volunteered to help me with my act. A big round of applause!'

She started clapping. I clapped as well and the sound echoed around the empty circus tent. Though it was only a rehearsal she was performing her little socks off.

'Naturally, we have to be prepared,' she announced. From behind the huge something she produced a crash helmet and handed it to Ho.

'Put this on!'

Ho shook his head and folded his arms. Maude raised her slapping hand once more.

Ho put on the helmet.

I, being the ever vigilant detective, was beginning to get suspicious. I sat forward in my seat.

Maude grasped the edge of the canvas sheeting which shrouded the enormous object.

'. . . Then the band go "Tra-laa!" and I pull off the cover.' And she did so.

The sheet fell from the huge something, revealing it to be a slightly worrying something. 'Twas the biggest cannon I had ever laid eyes on. A massive thing, rusty and well used. Looked like it could fire a projectile a fair distance.

Maude clapped her hands and a mumbling stagehand opened the flaps that formed the entry to the tent. Outside and far, far away I could just make out a small net. I gripped the arms of my seat.

'Now, if my nice, helpful volunteer would kindly climb up this small ladder.'

Ho was mumbling under his breath and fiddling with his helmet strap. He obviously wasn't happy, but he didn't want to be slapped again. Reluctantly, he placed a foot on the bottom rung.

Thoughts careered through my mind. Should I stop this? Did she know what she was doing? Did Ho know what *he* was doing? I was frozen to the seat.

The ladder was taken away as Maude produced a small box of matches and struck one.

'And now, ladies and gentlemen, you will behold a miracle as my kind volunteer is shot across the field into that tiny net!'

She clicked her fingers and the distant net was suddenly illuminated by two small floodlights.

As I sat dumbstruck, she produced a small box of matches and struck one, touched the fuse with the match and watched it blaze into spluttering life.

'You can't do that to my cook!' I yelled.

I pelted down the stairs at a rate of knots, leaped across the ring and over to the huge cannon. I pushed the ageing showgirl aside and began beating at the flame with my hat. I couldn't extinguish it. Maude tugged at my coat, but I tried to fight her off. However, she was a stronger wench than she appeared and, with one massive lunge, she pushed me against the cannon. It moved, shifting its position slightly. It no longer pointed at the net. Now it was pointing at . . .

'My office!' shouted Whackett, who had just reappeared. 'Don't aim it at my office!'

Maude struggled with me to re-aim the cannon . . .

BANG!!!!!

The cannon exploded with an ear-shattering report and my oriental cook whooshed through the air. He crashed through the office window, narrowly missing the octopus, who was still holding up the *A to Z*. Ho smacked his head against the open book and, finally, hit the wall. He crumpled in a moaning heap on the floor.

☠   ☠

It goes without saying that Whackett threw us out of the circus. We'd ruined two of his offices and this time we'd upset his octopus. Pah! All we had wanted was a measly crumb of a clue to set us back on course.

As for Ho, we put him to bed and the next the day he was fine. I knew he was fine because he started complaining again.

'A film star!' he said, scraping something off the cheese to make breakfast.

'What?' I asked.

'A film star could have been walking past Kowloon Bay and fished me out. I could be in Hollywood now, drinking pink champagne and driving a huge Cadillac.'

I was about to respond with an encouraging comment about our jolly yo-ho-ho life when something about Ho grabbed my attention.

'Ho?'

'What now?'

'What's that on your forehead?'

Molly and Spot gathered around. We stared at some curious markings that seemed to have been stamped on Ho's head.

'Looks like a road map,' said Molly, prodding him.

'You must have hit the Washed-upon-the-Beach *A to Z* the octopus was holding,' I added. 'And you hit it so hard it's imprinted itself on your head. But all the writing's backwards.'

Spot flew over, clutching the tiny mirror from his cage.

I held the mirror to Ho's forehead and then we could clearly read the words, stamped above his eyebrows:

Benbow Recreation Ground.

What was the meaning of this? Why had the octopus shown me the *A to Z*? Had this section of the map become printed on Ho's head by accident or had the octopus intended it? Was clever Octavius trying to tell us something?

Ho had been gazing quietly at himself in the mirror.

'There was no K!' he breathed.

'What?' I said.

He grabbed the bottom photocopy from the coffee table and pointed at the note scribbled on the mysterious hand.

'Listen, we thought it read *Benbo* Wrec and the K was on the other side of the hand. Well, the space is in the wrong place – it should read Benbow *Rec*.'

'What?'

'We've been looking for the wreck of the *Benbo*, when we should have been looking for the Benbow Rec . . .'

He jabbed a finger at his forehead.

'Short for Benbow Recreation Ground!'

CHAPTER THIRTEEN

'**C**uttlefish and barnacles!' I cursed as I stomped up the Naughty Lass's pathway in a huff. 'Fish cakes!'

I paused on the doorstep, clutching my bag of cheese, lost in thought. We all make mistakes, I told myself. So what if I fell asleep at the Benbow Rec? So what if the villains came whilst I was asleep? So what if the place was covered with red herrings?

Let me explain these muddled mutterings. Upon finding the map printed on good old Ho's forehead my trusty crew and I put our brilliant brains together. We decided the Benbow Rec was the place wherein lay our next clue. Someone had to spend the night there and 'twould be a dull and thankless job. So they chose me.

I set to the task like the good and grizzled pirate I am. Unfortunately, I had a slight cold and took one swig too many of Dr Trelawney's Registered Cold Remedy. Drowsiness overtook me and I slumped into a snoring heap behind the see-saws.

When I awoke I found the rec covered with red herrings – all nibbled. And tiny footprints, too. I could have kicked myself. Plain evidence the villains had visited the park for whatever reason, and slunk off.

Whilst I had been making a mental note to take lots of coffee on our next case, Spot had squawked loudly and pointed with his little wing.

A pile of earth crumbled away as I prodded it, revealing something very interesting. There, hidden under the soil, was a box. A long, thin box, in fact. A box which would be the perfect size to fit the Cut-glass Cutlass. A whirlpool of thoughts had swirled in my brain. I snatched open the box – but 'twas empty.

Then a sudden thought occurred. Maybe I hadn't slept through a *theft* last night. Maybe this was where the vile villains *stored* the cutlass once it had been stolen. And when they were ready to sell it again they'd come to fetch it. And they had come to fetch it last night. And I had missed it.

'Barnacles!'

Tired and cross from my nasty night in the rec, I kicked the doorstep of the Naughty Lass in frustration. Then I took a deep breath and slowly pushed open the front door.

All was still as a millpond. I tiptoed in. Nothing was a-stirring and all was as quiet as the ocean bed. Ho and Molly wouldn't be pleased with me falling asleep last night so I'd bought some flowers on the way. Well, I'd intended to buy some flowers, but the piffling florist was shut so I'd bought some cheese instead.

I crept into the hallway. 'Twas like a ghost ship. All the lights were on, but no one seemed to be home.

'Heave-ho!' I cried as heartily as I could. But no reply came.

'I've got cheese!'

I stepped into the lounge. No sign of Molly practising her archery. No sign of Ho doing something unusual with an egg. I pondered and wondered if I'd boarded the wrong ship. I released Spot from my pocket and he fluttered about the room. He came to rest on his anchor-shaped perch and his little head moved from side to side.

Then a strange and distant sound sailed into my shell-like. 'Twas some manner of bleeping sound. Electronic bleeping, at that. And it seemed to be coming from under my feet.

I carefully placed the cheese on the wonky coffee table and let my ears lead the way. I walked back into the hallway, where the sound grew a little louder. I put my ear to the cellar door. Ha! This was the place. I opened the door and slowly descended into the darkness. The bleeping grew louder as I went.

The cellar was a place for keeping old treasures and boxes and packing cases. 'Twas festooned with knickknacks and what-nots from my pirating days – a shrunken head from Africa, a didgeridoo from Australia, a chunk of molten rock from Iceland, a Kiss Me Quick hat from Blackpool. Oh, the memories. In the shadowy depths my deckhands, Ho and Molly, were huddled over a televisual box – a televisual box much smaller than the one upstairs.

'Ahoy, ship mates!' I cried, striding over to them.

'Shhhh!' they both said, neither taking their attention from the screen.

Suddenly Ho yelled,'You sunk my battleship!'

They both turned to look at me.

'Morning, boss!'

'Can't I leave you in charge of the Naughty Lass for five minutes? You should be on watch, to leap on any clues that drift our way, but here you are playing those bleep-bleep games. Sometimes I think you're as thick as two short plankton!'

Ho and Molly exchanged a glance and Molly said,'How did the stake-out go, boss?'

I nibbled a fingernail.

'I've got some cheese,' I said.

I explained about falling asleep, of course, and about waking the next morning to find all the red herrings, the tiny footprints and the buried box. I haven't become a noble sailor without learning when to bite the cannonball and tell the truth.

Ho dunked a chunk of cheese in his cocoa. 'But we need clues, boss! Duh!'

'I know we need clues! Do I look like an idiot . . . ?'

Molly was about to speak.

'Don't answer that! Answer this instead. While I was writhing in pain out in the cold, cold night, what were you two a-doing, eh? You were playing silly bleep-bleep games!'

I slurped my cocoa.

'No, we weren't,' said Molly.

'What?'

'We weren't playing computer games, boss.'

'But my beady eye spied you, my little whelk!'

'We were playing games when you *arrived*. But that was after we spent the entire night setting up a website for you.'

I slurped my cocoa again.

'A website, eh?' I scooped the skin from my cocoa with my finger.

'Oh, come on, Sam, follow me!' Ho grabbed my hand and led me to the computer, where he explained all about websites and how one could help our detecting business. People could use it to find out all about us. It was like advertising all over the world.

'So it's like a big notice board?' I asked.

'That's right, boss.' 'So why don't we just get a big notice board?'

Ho explained.

'Listen, boss, people in trouble will send emails to our website and we go and investigate – do you get it now!'

I was mightily impressed. I hadn't been this impressed since Jolly Joan, the landlady of the Chuckling Duckling, showed me how she could catch a lemon in her bellybutton.

'And all we do is wait!' Ho placed his hands behind his head, put his feet up and we waited.

And we waited.

And waited.

And waited.

My cocoa had gone stone cold by the time I said, 'Anyone emailed us yet?'

'Not yet, Sam. Be patient!'

And we waited some more.

'Twas about three o'clock in the afternoon when a thought crawled into my head. I stopped playing my squeeze-box mid-shanty and said, 'How do people know where to send their emails, Ho?'

Ho nearly fell off his chair. 'Oh, fish sticks,' he said. 'I forgot to put our address on the leaflets.'

I was about to burst out with some naughty nautical words, but Ho was already at work with the computer. Within minutes the printer was spitting out leaflets. I snatched one from the floor. 'Twas not a bad piece of parchment – on the front was a picture of your good captain, inside was a list of our charges, and on the back was our email address.

'Brilliant, Ho, brilliant. Now, who hands out the leaflets?'

They both looked at me in that way they have. I stuffed my sack with leaflets and traipsed off into town.

☠   ☠

'Twas another stunning sunny day in Washed-uponthe- Beach. I went from shop to shop handing out my leaflets and chatting to all and sundry. Soon all the leaflets were gone and I decided to phone the Naughty Lass and have them prepare some more. I yawned as I punched in our number and held the phone to my shell-like. Then something odd occurred – I heard two voices in conversation. One male, one female. I'd got what they call a crossed line. Now I know it's rude to eavesdrop on private conversations, but I am a detective and, who knows, it might get interesting.

This is what I heard:

Male: Do you have the money?

Female: I'm getting it.

Male: Mr X is very concerned no one learns about this.

Female: I'm not telling anyone!

Male: The price is £10,000 – half up front, half on delivery.

Female: You told me £8,000!

Male: There have been complications. The police have been investigating. There was a story about it on Police Watch *last night. Mr X was very annoyed.*

Female: And you're certain this is the Cut-glass Cutlass?

Male: It is the one and only Cut-glass Cutlass.

Female: So let me get this straight. You're offering the cutlass to me for £10,000 cash?

Male: Correct. Be at Lobster King at 4 p.m. Bring half the money – or no cutlass.

Female: How shall I recognize you?

Male: I shall be wearing a red rose.

Two clicks and the phone fell silent. I stared at it in amazement. A tidal wave of thoughts crashed into my brain. What was I to do? I looked at my watch – 3 p.m. Barnacles, I thought, there's only one thing for it. I jutted my jaw and set off for Lobster King.

☠   ☠

I stood below the giant plastic lobster and watched its frozen smile as it waved its huge claws. Beneath the lobster in enormous red letters were the words:

LOBSTER KING
Home of the Famous Six Squid Milkshake

The sun glinted off the shiny words. 'Twas a fast-food restaurant that sold all that junk food. Not the kind of nourishment I like to chomp, though. Still, 'twas my duty, so in I stepped.

Inside, the place was perfectly scrubbed from prow to stern and packed with gaggles of families, merrily munching their way through piles of fries and fishy burgers. I looked about for a seat, but there was none.

'What can I get you, sir?'

I turned to see a short, ginger-haired teenager dressed in bright red. He beamed at me. I pointed at what I thought was a menu. It was only later I found out it said 'Jobs Available Immediately'.

'I'll have one of those, please!'

'What, now?' said the youth.

'Certainly.'

The teenager smiled, grabbed my hand, whisked me into the back room of the restaurant and quickly fitted me for a uniform. Seemed a strange service to offer, but I went along for the ride.

'Have you ever served before?' asked the youth.

'I've served aboard the finest ships afloat!' I replied proudly.

'And can you work a till?'

'I've spent many hours at the tiller!'

'Good! Right, off you go, then!'

He gestured towards the restaurant and waiting customers. 'Twas at that point I realized I was no longer a customer — I was Lobster King's latest employee. I took a deep breath and jumped in.

Now I don't like to boast, but Old Hawkins mastered the menu within minutes and served away merrily. I even found time for a few nautical jokes as I went.

I was just scooping some Lobster Nuggets into a paper net when a strange character entered the restaurant. I couldn't make out her face as a scarf covered it, but her figure seemed oddly familiar. She slid into a plastic chair and glanced at her watch. I glanced at mine.

4 p.m.!

At that point another figure entered – a tall, gangling man with a face like a rocky outcrop and a body to match. As I gazed, I noticed something in his lapel. It was a red rose.

'Six Squid Milkshake!' said an irritating young voice.

I ignored it.

The woman waved the man over and he joined her at the table. They looked about and then entered into hushed conversation. If only I could hear what they were saying.

'A Six Squid Milkshake, puh-leaseee!'

After a few moments the woman produced a thick, brown envelope which she slid across the table.

I was handing the small child his Six Squid Milkshake when an idea occurred. I had to do something. I snatched the milkshake back from the child and bounded over to the couple at the table. I slapped the drink down in front of them, splashing the contents over the man and the woman.

'Somebody order a milkshake?'

The man wiped away the shake and stared up at me. He glanced at me twice, but didn't seem to recognize me. Suddenly, in a storm of huffing and puffing, he strode out of the restaurant – leaving behind the envelope.

'Oh, great, really great!'

It was the woman talking. She pulled the scarf from her face. It was the Mayor of Washed-upon-the-Beach – Lola Schwartz. And she looked furious.

'There I was with the criminal right in the palm of my hand and who should screw it all up? Sam Hawkins!'

'But, your lordship, your warship, your parsnip, I didn't know . . .' I blathered away, attempting to explain myself. Suddenly, a thought entered my mind.

'Wait a minute!' I said, sitting down. 'Why were *you* trying to buy the Cut-glass Cutlass? It's already been stolen from you once.'

'How did you know I was?' she said suspiciously.

I pulled out my mobile phone. 'Crossed line!' I explained. 'I heard you setting it all up.'

'Hawkins, I was doing a little entrapment!'

'A little what?'

'I was acting as bait to get the cutlass back and get the criminal as well.'

'To land two pilchards with one net!' I cried.

'Something like that. Look, the cutlass was stolen. I was in charge. I needed to show I wasn't a no-good mayor. So I tried to buy it back secretly. I knew the police would never find it.'

'Who offered it to you?'

'He was only called Mr X. The guy you just scared off was working for him.' She threw her arms in the air. 'But I almost had Mr X *and* the cutlass and then you blundered in and blew the whole scam out of the water.'

She punched the empty milkshake cup into the table with a squelch.

'Don't you realize my career depended on this? I could have been the best mayor this driftwood town had ever seen if you hadn't stuck your oar in! I could have been somebody! Now I gotta think up another plan!'

I sat down beside her, rather embarrassed, and patted her hand.

'Maybe I could help you . . .'

'No!' she screamed.

She grabbed the paper cup and began tearing it apart.

'You'll pay for this, Hawkins!'

'Well, it's only £2.50 . . .'

'Not the milkshake, you fool! You'll pay for the damage you've done to my career!'

With that, she tossed the scarf over her shoulder and stomped out of the restaurant, leaving behind nothing but a bad attitude and a whiff of expensive perfume.

I'd rather pay for the milkshake, I thought.

I felt a tugging at my apron. I looked down to see a small boy's face, gazing up at me like a trout at feeding time.

'He stole my milkshake!' he suddenly shouted to everyone in the restaurant and, standing on a chair, gave a hearty pull on my nose. I was incensed! Now I only had one choice – I kicked the chair from under him. He collapsed in a heap and his wailing drew the attention of the ginger-haired teenager.

'You're fired!' said the voice of the spotty boss who, not very long ago, had been so eager to employ me. He untied the apron from around my belly and pointed towards the door. 'Go away!'

And at that I left with my head held high. Partly due to pride and partly to stop my nose bleeding.

CHAPTER FOURTEEN

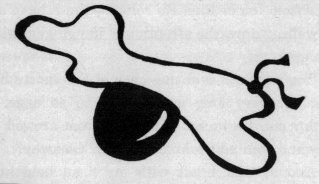

Back at the Naughty Lass I sat on my squeaky, creaky rocking chair with my squeeze-box on my lap and a large plaster on my nose. I was making a squid's dinner of this case and I knew it. I was thinking about throwing in the anchor. I was never going to find the Cut-glass Cutlass. I was all at sea – and not in a good way. Maybe I'm simply not cut out to be a detective after all, I thought. Maybe I should just give in now and never think about solving crimes again. I started to pump the squeeze-box and sing an old sea-shanty.

'I once had a porpoise, now where has it gone . . .?' I sang.

A knock came at the door and Ho's face peered in.

'What's up?' he asked gently.

'What am I going to do now?' I moaned, touching my aching nose. 'The only chance of getting my fingers on the cutlass has been blown sky high 'cos of my stupidity! The bloke in the restaurant saw my face! He didn't seem to recognize me, but he left without the money. The deal's off. I'll bet my breeches on it. Once he's seen one of our leaflets, the penny will plop.' I waved a leaflet at Ho – it had my grinning face on the front. I crumpled it and threw it away, putting my squeeze-box to one side. 'So what should I do?'

'Use your charms.'

I eyed Ho.

He explained further.

'Go and find the Mayor. Say sorry for upsetting her. Maybe there's some other way to get the cutlass delivered. Then when it arrives we grab the delivery person and question them!'

I gazed out over the fields behind the Naughty Lass, past the church at the clouds beyond, and pondered Ho's words. In the distance a seagull swooped.

'You can do it!' said Ho, standing.

'Do you really think so, Ho?'

'That's why you're the captain, Captain.'

And with that, Ho saluted me. I couldn't remember the last time he'd done that. I smiled a weak smile as he left the room.

All I had to do was to gather my charms in one net and set them before the Mayor. Couldn't be difficult – I'd wooed women afore. I remember Lazy Susan, from the Nag and Nose-bag – she held a candle for me for years after I sang her a sea-shanty. And when I left her at the dockside she gave me a little wave – I've still got it downstairs in a bucket. I have a way with the fairer sex. I could twinkle my eyes, smirk my cute grin and before long the Mayor would be in the palm of my hand. I've smuggled clams with the best of them! I could wrap the Mayor around my little finger if I set my mind to it.

I decided there and then to set my mind to it.

I leapt from the rocking chair.

'I'm going to have the Mayor falling at my feet!' I cried, and tripped over my squeeze-box.

I rang the doorbell of the Mayor's home. 'Twas one of those new blocks on the better side of town. I caught a glimpse of my reflection in a window. How could she resist the sight that would meet her eyes? I'd sprayed on a little Old Splice and even tied a ribbon in my hair.

The door was flung open and there stood the Mayor. She was dressed to perfection. A red dress wrapped her up like cling film. She looked like a woman who wanted to be wooed. She looked me up and down.

'Sam Hawkins.'

'Good evening,' I said in my most seductive voice, and twiddled my neckerchief.

'Goodnight,' she said, and slammed the door.

Luckily, I'd managed to jam my foot betwixt the door and the frame afore it fully closed.

'Get your scruffy foot out of my door, Hawkins!' she yelled, kicking my boot.

'Please, your ladyship. I beg you hear me out. I brought you this.'

There must have been something in my voice that made the Mayor open the door. She peered at me through the crack. I smiled a suave smile and she opened the door further.

'What have you brought me?'

I handed her the present and bowed courteously.

'A little something I grew myself,' I explained.

'Hawkins – these are nettles!' she said.

I leaned closer to her.

'Every time you look at them, think of me.'

'I shall,' she said, slamming them on the nearby table. She looked at me, took at deep breath and said, 'You'd better come in!'

Ha! Old Hawkins's smarmy charm had worked its magic. I slid into the Mayor's house as she quickly closed the door. She led me to the lounge, which was decorated with impeccable taste. Fine paintings, exquisite furniture, beautiful vases.

'So get to the point, Hawkins. What do you want?'

'Well, your ladyship, I've come to lay myself at your feet.'

The Mayor looked at her feet nervously. I continued.

'I've come to throw myself on your mercy. I've come to apologize.' I wriggled my eyebrows and grinned. 'My behaviour in Lobster King was unforgivable.'

'Yeah, I know.'

I cracked my knuckles in an irresistible way.

'But what do we care of such things? We have the moon, we have the stars . . .' I slid across the sofa towards her. She sat further back in her seat.

'But we don't have the cutlass.'

'Ah, but we will!'

I dropped to my knees before her.

'What are you doing, Hawkins?' she asked, looking worried.

Suddenly the phone burst into life. Keeping a steady eye on me, the Mayor reached across and snatched it.

'Yeah . . . tonight . . . thirty minutes . . . excellent . . .' She replaced the receiver and turned to me. 'Yesss!' she yelled, punching the air. 'The deal's still on. It's coming tonight!' She leapt to her feet and started chanting, 'Go, Lola! Go, Lola! Go, Lola!'

'But I thought the whole deal was off,' I said.

'So did I, but it seems Mr X has reconsidered. Trouble is, now he wants all the money on delivery. £10,000!'

'So?' I said.

'So I don't have £10,000!' She shrugged and flopped back in the chair. 'I only ever had half. I haven't had time to get hold of the rest.'

We sat in silence for a moment. Suddenly, I jumped to my feet and dusted down my knees.

'My Chinese cook is waiting outside!'

'Has he got £5,000?'

I had no answer to that, but we had to act fast. I dragged in Ho from the bushes outside. His camera was hanging from his neck. He moaned and complained as I found a convenient cupboard in which to squeeze him.

'See?' I said to the Mayor. 'When the person arrives with the cutlass, Ho leaps out and takes their photograph. Evidence, you see!'

'But what about the money?' pleaded the Mayor, looking at her watch.

I put my hand in my pocket – and a huge smile spread across my face.

'Oceanopoly!' I announced triumphantly, producing a wad of toy money. 'Still in my pocket from that night at Peg-nose Pedro's!' I wafted it before the bewildered face of the Mayor. She sighed very slowly.

'This isn't going to work, Hawkins!'

'Do I look like I don't know what I'm doing?'

Before she could answer, the doorbell rang. The Mayor stood up to answer it, but I pushed her aside.

'Leave it to the professionals!'

I threw open the door.

A staggering sight met my eyes. 'Twas like nothing I'd ever seen in all my years at sea. Before me, dressed as a pizza delivery person, was the circus octopus. I was lost for words.

'Ermmmm . . .' I said finally.

In his clammy tentacles the octopus was holding a giant pizza box. He offered it to me. I swiftly gathered my thoughts and cracked on with the plan.

'So this is the *Cut-glass Cutlass!*' I said, snatching the box from his tentacles.

At those words, Ho leaped from his hidey-hole and shot off a whole reel of flashy snaps. The octopus stood hypnotized by the flashing. In that instant I threw the pizza box towards the Mayor and then deftly grabbed the octopus.

Ho suddenly pointed at the octopus's tentacle.

'Tentacle!' he shouted. 'That's what I saw the other night at Peg-nose Pedro's!'

I grabbed a tentacle.

'So who's Mr X, you slimy sea creature?' I bent his tentacle. 'It's Whackett, isn't it?' The octopus continued staring into nothingness as I bent its tentacle further. 'He's trained you to steal the cutlass, hasn't he?' Just as I was considering tying a knot in the tentacle, the Mayor spoke.

'At last!' she said. 'It's finally back in safe hands!'

Ho and I turned to look at her. She had opened the mega-size pizza box. Nestling inside, wrapped in red velvet, was the Cut-glass Cutlass. I released the octopus from my vice-like grip and ran over to her. So did Ho.

There it was – just as I remembered it. Its fine craftsmanship. Its stunning curves and lines. It twinkled in the light, so pure and clean. The Cut-glass Cutlass. Mother would have been so proud of me.

'Excellent!' said Ho, and took a photo of it.

I looked up at the Mayor and a tear almost came to my eye.

'We've got the Cut-glass Cutlass,' I said.

'No, Sam Hawkins, *I've* got the Cut-glass Cutlass! And I've got to give Mr X £10,000 of

Oceanopoly money!' As she spoke, she stuffed a fat bundle of fake money into an envelope and shoved it into the octopus's outstretched tentacle.

'So what do I get?' I asked.

'You get the octopus! Goodnight!' And with that she bundled us all out of the door and slammed it behind us.

We stood on the pavement. The stars glistened above in the night sky and I sighed.

The octopus looked up at me sadly. I took the pizza delivery hat from its head and threw it into the bushes.

Ho and I shrugged at each other, took a tentacle each and made our way slowly home to the Naughty Lass.

☠ ☠

Molly and Spot were playing Scrabble when we arrived. Molly looked up as we entered the living room.

'That's an octopus – seven letters,' she said.

'Very good,' I said, collapsing in a chair. 'Go and put a duvet in the bath – he's staying the night.'

The octopus looked about the room. He seemed pleased to be there – or I think he was pleased. It's difficult to tell with an octopus. Anything had to be better than living in a circus and working for Whackett.

'What do octopuses eat, then, Sam?' asked Ho.

'Haven't the foggiest. Fish, probably.'

I shuffled over to the octopus and looked for an ear. I couldn't find one so I shouted slowly, 'DO . . . YOU . . . EAT . . . FISH?'

His dark eyes darted about and finally landed on the Scrabble board. He stretched his tentacle towards it and picked out three letters – Y, E, S.

'You really are a clever octopus, aren't you?' I said, amazed. 'Molly, Ho, come and see what the octopus did.'

Ho and Molly gathered around the board. Molly patted the octopus on the head. He wriggled slightly and snorted.

'Maybe we should ask more questions!' suggested Ho.

'Did you steal the Cut-glass Cutlass for your boss?' I asked.

Y, E, S.

'Did he force you to commit crimes against your will?'

Y, E, S.

'Did you nibble the red herrings?'

Y, E, S.

'And when the cutlass was stolen from all those nice innocent people, where was it hidden?'

The octopus selected some new letters. R, E, C.

'The Rec. The Benbow Recreation Ground! I told you there was a connection!' shouted Ho.

The octopus let out an exhausted sigh. But I had one last question to ask.

'Who is Mr X?' I said quietly.

There was silence. The octopus softly blinked its inky eyes. We waited for an answer, but it soon became clear that the octopus was too frightened to give us one.

'Very well,' I growled crossly, 'you can stay as silent as a fog-bound tug, but we'll soon find out the answer! Our next port of call will be the Benbow Recreation Ground! I must have missed a clue before, but this time I shall not!'

And, with a hearty 'yo-ho-ho', I led my flotilla of mates out of the Naughty Lass and towards our final goal.

CHAPTER FIFTEEN

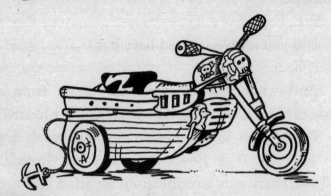

The Nippy Clipper – our speedy little motorbike and sidecar – sped along the country roads of Washed-upon-the-Beach at a fair rate of knots, with Molly, Ho, Spot, the octopus and me aboard. What would we find at the Benbow Rec? I pondered as we screeched around a corner. Would this be the answer to our mystery? The events of the past few days swam through my mind as I tried to figure out why the Rec could be so important.

Washed-upon-the-Beach blurred past. The wind was in our hair and a gaggle of seagulls flapped in our wake. What more could a merry pirate ask for?

Soon the Benbow Rec was in our sights. I slowed the bike to a decent pace and stopped near the park. I slipped my telescope from my sack and held it to my eye. In the fading light of the day, I could just make out a figure silhouetted against the setting sun – a tall, strong figure wearing what seemed to be a top hat. A top hat! Of course, who else could it be – 'twas Whackett himself, our chief suspect!

I left Ho and Molly by the Nippy Clipper and approached the gates of the Rec.

'Ahoy there!'

Whackett looked about him. He was holding a shovel.

'What the blithering heck do you want?' he snarled.

'Permission to board!' I yelled.

Whackett tried to hide the shovel, but failed. I pulled at the tall iron gate but 'twas locked. Tish! This was not the best way to make my grand entrance.

Within seconds, Ho, Molly, Spot and the octopus had seen my dilemma and were pushing and huffing and puffing to get my hulking body over the fence. Spot tugged at my neckerchief to help. I was finally heaved over and fell with a crunch into a bush. I stood up, stepped in a mole hole, dusted off my hat and approached Whackett.

He was standing by the children's playground, clutching his shovel to his chest. He was surrounded by hole after hole after hole. But these were not mole holes – these were holes dug by humans, and I was looking at the human who'd dug them.

He looked nervously from the holes to his shovel to me. Then his eyes fell on the octopus.

'What are you doing with my octopus? I could report you for this!'

I decided to get straight to the point. 'I accuse you of stealing the Cut-glass Cutlass!' I declared, pointing a finger at him.

'What did you say?' he said, stabbing the shovel into the ground and leaning on it.

'I saw the boots in your safe!' I said triumphantly.

He eyed me up and down as if I was a badly behaved puppy.

'No,' he sighed. 'I have not stolen the Cut-glass Cutlass. If I *had* stolen it I would be living a life of luxury in the South of France. If I *had* stolen it I wouldn't be digging holes in a children's playground in Washedupon- the-Beach!'

He had a point.

'So what *are* you doing?' I asked, looking around at the holes.

'I'm *looking* for the Cut-glass Cutlass!'

'Why do you think it might be here?' I asked casually.

'Because every time the cutlass is bought by someone, a few days later it's stolen.'

'Yes.'

'And when it's stolen, it's brought here.'

'How do you know?'

'Quite simple, Hawkins. The day after the cutlass was stolen from Peg-nose Pedro I was out here exercising my llamas.'

'Very nice,' I said politely, but I was eager for him to get to the point.

'As we trotted past the swings, I noticed red herrings all over the place. Red herrings and tiny footprints! And these things are always left behind whenever the cutlass is stolen.'

'I know that!' I said indignantly. 'I'm a detective. It took me days to work all that out!'

'Really? It was on *Police Watch* last night.' He kicked the soil at his feet. 'I've dug all over this area – been at it for hours – but I still can't find the cutlass.' He threw his shovel to the ground and muttered, 'I give in!'

He dropped to the ground next to his shovel and started to blubber like a baby. He produced a handkerchief from his pocket and blew a clarion blow into it.

I wasn't quite sure what to do at this point, so I said what all pirates say in such awkward situations.

'Would you like a cup of tea?'

☠   ☠

Back at the Naughty Lass, Whackett stared, red-eyed, into his teacup and tried to identify its contents. He stirred it, sipped it and pulled a face like a worried heron.

'No tea, thank you.' He produced the handkerchief from his pocket and blew into it once more. 'You don't understand – I just want to make some money. Just a little bit of money – for once in my life.'

Molly and Ho sat on the settee twiddling their thumbs – not each other's, of course, their own – and on the floor sat the octopus with Spot on his head.

'But what about the midget lookalikes?' I said, removing the teacup and emptying its contents into a small Venus flytrap plant which stood on the windowsill.

Whackett looked mournful and blew his nose again.

'Left me! Left me for a better manager! They were offered more money and off they went.'

The Venus flytrap spat out the tea ungratefully. Goodness knows what Ho had made it from. I placed a hand on Whackett's shoulder.

'There, there,' I said, and added, 'Never mind.'

'That's why I'm looking for the Cut-glass Cutlass. I could sell it and make a fortune.'

'But we thought you were stealing it and selling it to collectors – the museum, Lady Booming-Clapshot, Peg-nose Pedro.'

'Not me. I wasn't doing the stealing or the selling. That was Mr X!'

'Who is Mr X?'

'I don't know. I've only ever met people who've worked for him. But I used to rent the octopus to him.'

'*What?*

'I used to rent the octopus to him and four pairs of the midgets' boots.'

'The mist is clearing. So Mr X used to steal the cutlass and when he'd got it he'd sell it again to someone else!'

The octopus nodded excitedly, dislodging a squawking Spot from his perch.

'But how did he use the octopus?'

'This is the finest octopus I ever owned.' Whackett looked quite emotional. He sat on the arm of the settee and took a tentacle. 'I trained him to climb up ladders and walls and all sorts of things! Every time he did well, I gave him a herring. Always his favourite type – the red ones!'

'So you rented a highly trained and athletic octopus to Mr X together with four small pairs of boots!'

'Exactly! He used to pay me £4,000 every time he used them!'

'£4,000?' I immediately remembered Whackett's account book.

'It's the best octopus in the business!' he went on.

'And ideal as a thief!'

The octopus was banging the floor in agreement with his tentacles. 'Twas clear he hadn't enjoyed his time with the mysterious Mr X or being an octopus for rent. Now he knew he was amongst friends.

'But what did he use the little boots for?'

'I never worked that out,' said Whackett, sadly returning the tentacle to the octopus. At which point the octopus reared up like a stallion, scuttled across to me and started pointing wildly at my feet, then at Whackett's and then at Molly's and Ho's.

I felt the anchor drop with that loudest plop I'd heard so far.

'Everyone – take off your boots!'

Within moments, four pairs of boots sat side by side on the floor of the Naughty Lass. Whatever was our slimy little friend up to?

Slowly and very, very carefully, the octopus slipped a tentacle into one of the boots, followed by another and then another until a boot sat at the end of all eight tentacles. He walked about a little to demonstrate his point.

'So Mr X made the octopus wear little shoes deliberately so they'd leave tiny footprints, making us think the midgets did it!'

The octopus collapsed in a heap and sighed. His job was done. Molly and Ho patted him on the head and prised their shoes off him.

Whackett came and sat by me at the table. Another thought had occurred to me.

'But if Mr X is to steal the cutlass again, he'll need the octopus and the boots.'

'Sadly, that's where you're wrong. Look!'

Whackett slid a fax from his pocket and pushed it across the table to me. I unfolded it and read:

Whackett! Keep your octopus and keep your boots!
I no longer need them. Our contract is cancelled.
Mr X.

I folded the fax and handed it back.

'But why?'

I said.

'Duh!' said Ho, looking at the fax. 'It's obvious – Mr X has begun to realize that people are associating the red herrings and the tiny footprints with his thefts. It was even on the telly. So he's changed his methods.'

'That's right!' I cried. 'I wondered how long it would take you to work that out!'

Ho slumped back in the settee and silence fell across the room. The clock tick-tocked in the corner as we all pondered the new information.

I suddenly sat up and slapped the table.

'No, no, wait a mo, pal. You were digging in the rec because you'd seen a report of the cutlass being stolen from Peg-nose Pedro?'

'That's right!'

'But haven't you heard?'

'Heard what?'

'The cutlass has been sold on again since then. The Mayor has got it. It's at her house. And she hasn't even paid for it. Mr X will want to get his criminal claws back on it'

Whackett leaned forward as I continued.

'The cutlass hasn't been hidden at the Rec because,' I spoke slowly, realizing the weight of my words, '. . . it hasn't been stolen again yet!"

'Slop buckets!' he shouted.

'The Mayor has the cutlass, matey, and it won't be hidden at the Rec again until it's stolen from her!'

'So what are we going to do?'

I leaped on to my chair triumphantly.

'We must get to the Mayor's house before Mr X!'

And with that I herded my heroic crew back aboard the Nippy Clipper and kick-started it with glee.

CHAPTER SIXTEEN

Duh, *duh, duh, duh, duh!*
'Ho, that noise is really getting on my nerves!' I said as we tore along the roads of Washedupon- the-Beach.

'It's not me, Sam! We're being followed!' Ho replied.

I glanced into the rear-view mirror of the Nippy Clipper and a cold sweat broke out on my neck. 'Twas those blithering, landlubbing coppers Stump and Stibbins again! Didn't they realize the villain behind the theft of the Cut-glass Cutlass was almost in my net – I wasn't going to be stopped now.

The police car came alongside.

'Pull over!' mouthed Stibbins.

Molly looked at her holey sweater and put up two thumbs. I put my foot down and took the lead again.

After a few screeched corners, a number of terrified cats and a bewildered hedgehog, the Mayor's house came into view. 'Twas a welcome sight. We came to a halt outside and disembarked rapidly.

The police car came to a halt behind us and the two sweating officers clambered out.

Stibbins adjusted her tie, ran her hand through her greasy hair and approached us.

'Where's the fire, buster?' she asked crossly.

'I am Sam Hawkins, Pirate Detective, and I'm in pursuit of the villain who stole the Cut-glass Cutlass!' I explained.

'Of course you are, sir,' she said, making a funny face at Stump.

'The Cut-glass Cutlass is at the home of our honourable Mayor. We have reason to suspect it could be stolen from under her nose this very evening.'

'I see, sir.' Stump and Stibbins rolled their eyes at each other. They obviously didn't believe a word I was saying. I had to think quickly.

'And any police officer involved in netting the criminal responsible would be sure of a promotion.'

Stump and Stibbins exchanged a different sort of look.

'We're right behind you, sir!' they chorused.

With my ever expanding crew in my wake (Molly, Ho, Spot, Whackett, the octopus and officers Stump and Stibbins), I bounded up the driveway and rat-a-tat-tatted on the Mayor's front door.

After a few awkward moments the door opened. The Mayor stood there in her pink dressing gown with her hair in curlers, looking like a retired mermaid. She surveyed the motley crew on her doorstep.

'Is it Halloween already?'

I hastily explained the situation and she ushered us in. After she'd made sure none of the neighbours had seen us, she closed the door.

We clattered into the living room – and all stopped at the sight that met our eyes. There was the Cut-glass Cutlass, looking resplendent and beautiful in the twinkling moonlight. However, it was stabbed into a huge lump of cheese over by the wall.

'Look, I've decided to set a trap,' explained the Mayor.

'But that's what *we* do!' said Ho, more than a little disappointed.

'Yeah, and with your track record in catching the thief that would really have worked!'

Stump and Stibbins laughed at her sarcastic remark.

'And you two aren't much better!'

They stopped laughing.

'You should leave this to the professionals,' I said, twiddling my neckerchief and smiling.

The Mayor grabbed me by the neckerchief and dragged me towards her fuming face.

'Look, I haven't paid for this cutlass. Mr X is going to be a very, very unhappy man.'

'So unhappy he'll come and steal it back!' I said brightly.

'Exactly, so that's why I've set a trap! The villain climbs in through the window, grabs it and I grab them. And this better work, otherwise I'll never get re-elected!'

She released me and I doffed my hat apologetically.

PC Stibbins took my hat from my hand and placed it back on my head. 'But how will you capture the villain?' she asked.

The Mayor seemed a little befuddled and sat down.

'I'm a mayor – I open garden fêtes. You're the police, you're the detectives. You tell me!' she said huffily.

At this point, Ho and Molly huddled together and started muttering excitedly. Ho came over to me.

'We need to go back to the Naughty Lass,' he said, adding, 'We've got a plan, Sam!'

I granted permission and they scampered off into the night.

'Right,' I said, cracking my knuckles. 'To work!'

It took us a whole hour to complete the trap. Stibbins and Stump nipped back to the station and returned with armfuls of surveillance equipment, which they placed in various pots and vases throughout the living room. These camera things were all well and good, but they weren't going to capture the criminal, were they? We needed to grab the villain good and proper.

At this point, Molly and Ho returned dragging a large sack, which they dumped on the floor and slowly untied. Inside was a huge trawling net. 'Twas the one used by No-teeth Mackintosh, the whistling buccaneer, to collect his plunder. Now we would use it to collect ours! Yo-ho-ho! I could smell the salty sea breeze once more. At last I was back at the helm of an adventure!

But how were we to rig up the net?

I looked towards the Cut-glass Cutlass and then my eyes were drawn to what was directly above it – a large, stuffed moose's head. Ho looked at the moose's head.

I looked at Ho. We looked at each other. We both grinned and shook hands.

The Mayor shook her head in despair.

Before long, Ho and I had rigged the perfect trap. The net was tied to the moose's head. A long rope was attached to the net with a nautical slip knot. One yank and the entire net would descend and safely ensnare whatever shark was swimming below.

Now we had to hide.

'Twas not the largest bathroom in the world.

'I wasn't expecting to accommodate so many people,' explained the Mayor with a shrug.

I stood by the slightly open door, holding on to the end of the rope. Ho was by my side, squeezed next to the laundry basket. Molly was wedged between the bath and the sink, and the octopus sat on the toilet. Stibbins and Stump had no choice but to stand in the bath. Whackett and the Mayor were sitting under the basin.

What a rag-bag bunch we must have looked, but all the best ships are run by a varied selection of swabbies, each bringing their own skills and talents to the task in hand. I looked about the room at them all and wondered what skills they had. My eyes fell on the octopus, who looked sad and lonely and a little nervous. Stibbins and Stump were new crew members and I'd yet to ascertain their skills, but in the final moments of the catch they would be there to help reel in our prize. They also had a tiny televisual box which showed them a picture of the cutlass in the adjoining room. When someone approached the cutlass, they'd give me the sign and I'd tug my rope.

I looked over to Whackett, who was chatting to the Mayor. I knew he wasn't the criminal I had suspected him to be, but I'd still trust him no further than I could spit a pilchard. Ho and Molly were the finest sea persons you could ask for. My adventure wouldn't be complete without them.

With these thoughts splashing through my brain, we waited. Like a mousetrap ready to snap, like a harpoonist ready to fire, like a flying fish ready to . . . well, you get the idea.

We waited and waited.

Suddenly, and without warning, we heard a window smash.

The Mayor was about to curse, but Whackett placed a finger to her lips.

I glanced over to Stibbins and Stump, who were gazing, transfixed, at the little box in their hands.

'I can see movement!' whispered Stibbins.

We held our breath.

'Five figures moving around slowly.'

Five? I thought. Hope they've got enough handcuffs.

'Four small ones and one full-sized one. They've all got torches. They're getting closer to the cutlass . . .'

No one breathed.

'Now!' yelled Stibbins, and I gave a hearty yank on the rope.

Nothing happened.

I gave another yank.

Nothing happened again.

Suddenly, all hands joined me on the rope and we tugged with all our might. Finally, the rope leapt from our hands. In the room below we heard a crash and some muffled yelps.

We burst from the bathroom and headed for the living room.

☠   ☠

The Mayor slapped on the light switch as we gathered in the doorway.

'I am Sam Hawkins, Pirate Detective . . .' I started to announce.

The sight we saw was not what we expected. Wriggling like minnows in the net were four midgets – the lookalike midgets who had once worked for Whackett.

We stood open-mouthed. These four were the villains?

Stibbins and Stump swiftly disentangled them and handcuffed each one. The little people protested wildly as they did so.

'We are not villains!' they screamed together.

'These are my new midgets!' shouted Whackett. 'So this is better than being in a tribute band, is it? Bingo? Smartie? Zappo? Netto?'

'What are you doing here?' I asked them.

'We've been press-ganged,' said one of the four.

'Press-ganged?'

'Forced into doing something we didn't want to do by a beastly bad man,' said one of them. 'Please get this parrot off me!'

'But press-ganged by whom?'

From outside a voice bellowed. 'Twas a very, very familiar voice.

'Doh you dink you've caught me, eh?'

We looked astern and there, leering in through the broken window, was the snarling face of Peg-nose Pedro.

'Well, dat is where you're wrong!' he spat.

In his hand he brandished the Cut-glass Cutlass!

'I have da cutladd and you're dot getting it back!'

He waved the cutlass in the air, narrowly missing his Peg-nose.

'Pah – you dink you are cleverer than Peg-node Pedro, do you?'

I stepped forward a few paces, but Peg-nose held me at bay with the cutlass.

'But Peg-nose, someone already stole the cutlass from you!' I said, feeling very confused.

'*I* dole the cutladd from me, you dope, to put you off the dent!'

'What *dent*?' I asked, confused.

'I think he means scent, Sam,' hissed Ho helpfully.

'Enough! Follow me at your peril!'

And with that, Peg-nose Pedro whirled around and made off. We ran to the doorway.

In the road outside we saw Peg-nose leap aboard the Nippy Clipper and attempt to kick-start it. Ho suddenly whistled loudly. Peg-nose looked up angrily and saw Ho waving the bike keys at him. He quickly dismounted.

'Dat's not funny!' he yelled.

Ho threw the keys in the air triumphantly. Just as he tried to catch them as they descended, they slipped through his little hands into a nearby drain. There was a splosh below.

'Dat's funny, though!'

'After him!' yelled Stibbins, searching for her police whistle.

We were about to rush at Peg-nose when an icecream van turned the corner, playing a merry tune and looking for customers. Peg-nose flagged it down.

I heard nothing of their conversation, but saw Pegnose grab a cornet and make threatening gestures with it. The ice-cream man slowly began to climb out of the driver's seat and on to the pavement. Peg-nose, the villainous villain, leapt aboard and revved the engine.

What could we do? Ho had lost the keys to the Nippy Clipper and Peg-nose Pedro was making off with the Cut-glass Cutlass. Cuttlefish!

Spot was suddenly pecking at my ear. I tried to waft him away, but he became more insistent. I looked at my little birdy friend – in his claws he was holding some keys. Keys to the police car!

'Right!' I said to Stump and Stibbins. 'You interrogate the midgets and we'll get after Peg-nose!'

Before they had time to complain, Molly, Ho, Spot and I were out of the door and into the police car. I switched on the siren, turned the key and the engine roared like a hungry sea lion. We were away.

We hurtled through the streets of Washed-uponthe- Beach after our villain. But where was this black-hearted deckhand leading us?

Where indeed . . .

CHAPTER SEVENTEEN

The sun broke across the sky like a fridge door opening, as three piratical heroes and one piratical parrot sped along the High Street in the police car. Early-morning shoppers scurried for cover as we lurched through the streets of Washedupon- the-Beach; shops sped past at a rapid rate of knots, and we didn't even stop for red lights. Hee, hee!

Spot was desperately clinging to my shoulder. As we screeched around corners he grabbed at my earring. Molly sat in the back, hugging the headrest and grinning madly through the windscreen.

Ah, this was the life for a pirate. I had not moved at such break-neck speed since the time I was accidentally lashed to a dolphin. Ho, ho – a pirate's life for me.

I began to sing – 'Yo-ho-ho and a bag of clams . . .'

Molly placed her grubby hand across my mouth, silencing me. She pointed up ahead. A huge neon sign loomed before us:

LEISURE ISLAND

'Twas one of those theme park things, near Whackett's Circus, and later today was its grand opening. It looked as dull as a slop bucket to me, but I had a professional interest as the theme of the park was the 'Bubbling Blue Briny'. Every ride had something to do with the ocean. I also had another professional interest in it, for shooting through the gates was the ice-cream van. Aboard it was the mad and crazy criminal, Peg-nose Pedro.

The barrier snapped in two clean parts as Peg-nose shot through. A skinny guard poked his head out of his hut to inspect the damage, sighed, then poked his head back in as we approached.

We slowed as we neared the entrance and passed under the giant 'Leisure Island' sign.

I shouted, 'We're after him!'

'Have a nice . . .' replied the guard as we passed.

Leisure Island was a maze. 'Twas as simple as that. Roads and avenues shot off in all directions. All had different names – Mediterranean Way, Atlantic Walk, Caspian Avenue.

But which one to take? Where had Peg-nose gone?

Eagle-eyed Spot noticed a dollop of raspberry sauce at the mouth to Pacific Street, and we made off down it.

We slowed the police car and drifted down the street.

At this hour of the morn 'twas as deserted as the wreck of the *Hesperus*. Empty in an eerie way. Everything was new and all the shops and arcades sat silent, like unwrapped Christmas presents.

Molly pointed up ahead. The ice-cream van was parked and its engine was chugging quietly. It didn't take a brilliant detective to realize the van was empty.

'The van's empty,' I said.

'So where's he gone?' asked Molly.

I cupped a hand over my eyes and scanned the area. Ho did the same with his telescope. Suddenly he pointed. There, next to the Moby Duck Shooting Gallery, was a door with a broken lock and it was slightly ajar. I looked at the sign above:

HAUL OF MIRRORS

We crept in.

Now I don't know whether you've ever been in one of these places, but 'twas a strange and unsettling thing. Nothing more than a collection of mirrors, you understand, but not normal mirrors. Oh, no. These were fun mirrors — mirrors that were curved and so distorted anything reflected in them.

As I stepped into the first room I caught sight of a figure over my shoulder. I whipped around and found myself staring into the eyes of a distinguished-looking man in a pirate hat.

'Morning,' I said and raised my hat. So did he.

Molly and Ho pointed out my error as they stood behind me and in front of me at the same time, if you see what I mean.

In the next room we heard a crash. I leapt forward and my crew followed in my wake.

I couldn't believe my eyes. Peg-nose Pedros were everywhere. I counted thirteen at least. Standing perfectly still and waiting.

I paused in the doorway.

'I dow what you're dinking!' said Peg-nose, his nasal voice echoing through the hall. 'You're dinking, which is da real Pedro?'

Spot quietly left my shoulder.

'You're doh dupid, Dam Hawkins. I have the Cutgladd Cutladd. You have *dothing*!'

During this speech I noticed my old birdy pal slowly investigating each Pedro. He flew quietly to each and tried to land on its shoulder. I watched him from the corner of my eye, trying to work out what he was up to – then the anchor dropped. If he slipped, he knew it was a mirror. If he landed safely he knew 'twas Pedro! Brilliant bird. Very well trained, of course.

'And *dothing* is what you deserve! I'm warning you, Hawkins – don't interfere with me . . .' Pedro suddenly screamed. 'Get de bird off my dose!'

Spot had found the real Pedro. We stepped forward, as did all our reflections.

Pedro suddenly grabbed Spot's tiny body and held the Cut-glass Cutlass to his throat. 'Get off my dose!' he growled.

Slowly, very slowly, Spot released the nose and smiled nervously at Peg-nose.

Peg-nose threw us a sneering glance as he held Spot by the neck.

'Dam Hawkins, you have haunted me dince childhood! I've tried to become a good upstanding pirate and every dingle time you foil my plan. You annoyed me ad a child and you annoy me ad a man. I've had it up to 'ere wid you.' He indicated a height around his forehead. He looked like he was saluting. I almost saluted back. 'Tricking the police id fun, but tricking you id impoddible . . .'

'I know,' I said, proudly adjusting my collar.

'. . . becod you're doh dupid!'

He held the Cut-glass Cutlass to Spot's quivering throat once more.

'Dis is my final revenge, Hawkins – I take the cutladd, and with it I will 'lice your parrot in two!'

With that he backed away out of sight, keeping a beady eye on us and a tight grip on Spot.

What were we to do? If we followed he'd do his dastardly deed, but if we didn't follow we'd lose the Cut-glass Cutlass.

'We'll follow!' I finally decided. 'It's what Spot would have wanted.'

A single parrot feather on the ground led us to the gaping fire exit.

Out in the bright sunlight of early morn we looked about to see where Peg-nose had gone with our parrot.

We needn't have worried. Spot was sitting in a daze on the ground, fanning himself with his wing.

I scooped him up in my arms and hugged him.

'Which way did he go?' I asked.

Spot came out of his daze long enough to point a wing towards another attraction.

'Twas at this point I heard a voice. Not a human voice, but a voice which sounded like one of those fangling computer things.

'Wow!' cried Ho. 'That's amazing!' He was standing before the attraction at which Spot had pointed. On the front was a large plastic pirate. How they get away with these things I'll never know. It had a big plastic beard and a plastic sword that moved up and down automatically. With each swipe of the sword it spoke.

'Book in 'ere, you buccaneers! Book in 'ere, you buccaneers! Book in 'ere, you buccaneers!'

'Book in where? I don't understand,' I said.

Molly pointed at a sign that told us all we needed to know:

MADAM TWO-SWORDS' HOUSE OF JACKS

Suddenly, the mechanical pirate spoke again.

'All the latest pirate rowboats! All the latest pirate rowboats!'

'Thank 'ee,' I said, as we ducked under the turnstile and entered.

The first room was a sight to behold. 'Twas an old hang-out of mine, one the most popular taverns on the south coast – the Drunken Sailor.

All around us were pirates, mates I knew from my years at sea – Planky Frank, the cockle rustler; Bandy-legged Irene; the terror of the Thames; and Skull-faced McManus, who once swallowed a boot. It brought a tear to my eye to look upon my old friends once more. The place was just as I remembered it – dark and dusty, with sawdust scattered across the floor and a faint smell of ferrets. Oh, the good old days.

But what was wrong with them all? They were frozen. Frosty smiles were sliced across their faces and their eyes didn't move.

I slapped a hearty hand across the back of Musket Maureen, but she didn't move.

'So where are these rowboats, then?' I asked her.

She didn't reply.

Ho suddenly piped up. 'He didn't say "rowboats", Sam, he said "*robots*". These are mechanical versions of the most famous pirates in history.'

I looked about and sniffed.

'Most famous pirates in history, eh?'

'That's right, boss.'

I scanned the frozen gaggle of familiar faces and attempted to find the most famous face of all.

'So where am I, then?'

Molly stepped forward and placed a hand on my shoulder.

'Well, perhaps they're just *some* of the most famous pirates in history, boss.'

'Hmm, maybe,' I said, and changed the subject. 'So if they're robots, why aren't they moving?'

As those words left my lips, the entire complement of the Drunken Sailor burst into life. A tinny seashanty pumped out from a nearby table where Planky Frank and Musket Maureen were playing poker. Playing the same card over and over again, in fact. Behind Maureen, Jolly Roger, the barman, was cackling madly and drinking the same tot of rum again and again. The laughter was hollow and heartless, not like the old days. Behind the bar, Gold-tooth Mick was endlessly slicing bread with a sabre.

'And people find this amusing, do they?' I asked, looking at my noble band of brothers and sisters.

'Yes!' giggled both Molly and Ho.

My eyes were drawn to a mechanical version of Peg-nose Pedro. This dummy had been put in a triumphant pose in front of a large ship's wheel.

'Oh, I see he gets a place here, then.' I sniffed again.

Suddenly the robot spoke.

'Dat is just what I deserve!' it said.

'Cor,' I scoffed, 'it doesn't sound much like him.'

'I am da greatest pirate in history!' the robot said.

I noticed it was holding a perfect reproduction of the Cut-glass Cutlass.

'They're right up to date with these robot things,' I said. The version of Pedro was certainly more animated than the others.

'It's me, you idiot!' it said, waving the cutlass in the air.

I turned to speak to Molly and Ho, but they were no longer behind me.

'I am the *real* Peg-nose Pedro and dobody will take the Cut-gladd Cutladd from me!'

A thought entered the back of my nautical brain. It dragged itself out of the backwaters, towelled itself down and stumbled to the front of my mind. Could this be the *real* Peg-nose Pedro?

'It's me!' squealed the robot furiously. How realistic could these robots be?

And where were Molly and Ho when I needed them?

The robot grabbed its peg and rotated it in the taunting way for which Peg-nose was famous.

'Look! I rotate my dose!'

A cold sweat appeared on my brow. Could this be the real Peg-nose Pedro? The cold sweat slowly became a warm sweat as I spied Molly and Ho creeping up behind Peg-nose.

'You're not the *real* Peg-nose!' I suddenly cried, grasping the plan.

'Des I am!' screamed Peg-nose, furiously brandishing the cutlass.

Ho was slowly emerging from behind the ship's wheel in front of which stood Pedro.

'If you are the real Peg-nose Pedro, show me the scars on your belly where I poked you with a lobster when we were kids!'

Peg-nose pulled up his black tunic, revealing two deep scars.

'Dee?'

Ho had now clambered on top of the wheel and was leaning across to Pedro, with his legs held secure by Molly. Ho's fingers were stretching towards the Cut-glass Cutlass. He needed just a few more seconds. Just an inch or two more.

Suddenly there was a very loud and very long creak.

Peg-nose spun around to see Ho clawing for the cutlass.

The wheel creaked again under the combined weights of Ho and Molly. Something snapped. The wheel tumbled forward on top of Pedro, and the cutlass leaped from his grasp. It flew through the air and embedded itself in the head of Musket Maureen.

I had to get the cutlass! I strode over to the poker table and tugged at it, apologizing to Maureen as I did so.

'Worse things happen at sea, dear!' I said, and, with one final tug, the cutlass was free.

'I have the Cut-glass Cutlass!' I bellowed triumphantly and whirled around. At long, long last the Cut-glass Cutlass had found its rightful owner. Me.

But wily Peg-nose had dragged himself from under Ho, Molly and the wheel. He stood with Ho's head clenched under his arm – and a pistol aimed straight at him.

'Don't move – or your little cabin boy will be blasted to smithereens!'

All fell silent. We looked at each other.

He started to move away with Ho under his arm. Molly and I slowly followed him. He led us out of the Drunken Sailor. Why was he doing this?

The attraction next door was *Around the World in Five Minutes*. 'Twas a balloon ride. Ten large blue hotair balloons were tethered to a track which dragged the balloons over a map of the globe.

Peg-nose headed towards it, with Ho trembling under his arm. He straddled the fence and struggled to get Ho over too.

We followed slowly.

He pulled Ho towards one of the balloons, threw open the gate to the basket beneath the balloon and climbed aboard.

'You have the cutlass, I have the cabin boy!' he cackled.

Ho squealed in pain.

'Want to make an exchange?' he spat.

I inched forward. The cutlass glistened in my hand. What was I to do?

'Don't give it to him, Sam!' shouted my loyal cook.

Peg-nose pushed the pistol into Ho's head. 'Quiet!' he screamed.

I made my decision.

I stepped forward and held aloft the Cut-glass Cutlass with the hilt towards Peg-nose.

Pedro snatched it from my grasp and booted Ho from the basket. He landed in a heap at my feet.

'Ha – the cutladd id mine!' Pedro yelled, and, with four slicing splices, cut the ropes tying the balloon.

Slowly, it started to rise.

CHAPTER EIGHTEEN

I t kept rising higher and higher. Its huge shadow seeped across the pavement, covering Molly, Ho and me.

Peg-nose Pedro leaned from the basket above and taunted us with his nose-turning trick.

'I have da cutladd! I have da cutladd!' he chanted.

There have been times in my aquatic life when I've just wanted to give up. Like the time I was set upon in an alley by Press-gang Polly or the time I lost my stock of mussels in a game of Prussian Roulette. Well, this was another one of those times.

I turned to the others and said, 'Well, that's that, then, my watery pals. We've done our utmost and, like the honourable sailors we are, 'tis time to admit defeat.'

I dusted down my jacket, reshaped my hat and pulled myself together.

'I suppose we'd better return the police car.'

It was at this point that the situation changed.

'All aboard for a trip around the world!'

'Twas another of those faddling computer voices again. I turned to see another large balloon taking the place of the first one on the track. The gate to the basket opened like a hungry whale.

'All aboard for a trip around the world!' it repeated.

The crew of the Naughty Lass stood for a moment as we considered our next move. Molly was the first to speak.

'Let's follow him in that balloon! All we need do is climb aboard, untie the ropes and we could be after the cutlass!'

I fingered my neckerchief nervously. 'Come on, Sam, what's wrong?' asked Ho.

'Oh, blowholes!' I finally exclaimed. 'I can't go in that balloon!'

Ho and Molly looked at each other and then at me.

'Why?' they asked together.

"Cos I can't stand heights! Heights are my worst nightmare. I get queasy standing on tiptoe. Widths I can cope with, but not heights. Curses! What are we to do?'

Now Molly and Ho rarely lay a finger on their old captain, but on this occasion they chose to manhandle me aboard the balloon before I could protest.

'I'll be sick!' I warned them as they bundled me towards the basket.

They took no notice as they joined me inside it. They slammed the gate shut and began untying the ropes. Within minutes the basket shifted and so did my stomach. It swayed back and forth in the opposite direction to my knees. Oh dear. I peered out from behind my hands and watched as the land slipped away. I felt queasy. Oh dear, oh dear. But I had to be brave for my crew – I had to pull myself together and take command. I had to hold my head high and be proud and gallant like the noble sailor I was. I was sick over the side.

When I looked up again I spied Peg-nose's balloon ahead. We had some distance to gain, but at least we were in pursuit.

'How do we steer this thing, then, Captain?' asked Ho. 'Twas a good question to which I wished I had a good answer. It seemed obvious these balloons were nothing more than fairground attractions, never intended for real flight. We could end up anywhere. But I had to keep my worries from Ho.

'Ah, 'tis quite simple, my little crew mate. 'Tis merely a matter of . . . of . . .'

'We need some sort of propeller,' said Molly.

'. . . of some sort of propeller,' I finished.

The land was spreading out below us and, despite my heightophobia, 'twas a splendid view of the town. It lay below us like a huge road map. Leisure Island could be seen in all its glory, and next to it, like a dolphin calf nestling by its mother, was Whackett's Circus. Far in the distance I could spy Clapshot Towers. Nearby was the town square and the museum, and beyond that a small row of terraced houses, one of which was the Naughty Lass.

Ho was flapping his hat wildly.

'It's the closest I can get to a propeller!' he mumbled.

'Twas at this moment I made an unsettling discovery. If the town was becoming further away, the only thing that could take its place was . . .

'The sea! We're heading out to sea!' Molly yelled, pointing.

I felt queasier still.

'And so is Peg-nose Pedro!' she added.

I glanced towards our adversary and he, too, seemed a little concerned by the direction the balloons were taking. He kept rotating his nose at us, but now with less enthusiasm.

The chopping waves crashed and splashed below. I'd never seen the sea from this height and 'twas an awesome sight – what a mighty beast the ocean was!

Spot emerged from under my hat and attempted to solve our steerage problem. He grasped a guy rope in his little beak and began flapping towards Peg-nose's balloon.

Ho and Spot flapped their hat and wings respectively, but it made little difference. Even Molly flapping her arms failed to add any extra speed.

'We're hot on your heels!' I bellowed towards Pegnose. 'Keep flapping!' I hissed at the crew.

From his basket, I could just make out Peg-nose's words.

'You will never catch me in dat dupid balloon!'

I cupped my mouth.

'Wait and see!'

'You won't catch me, because you're too heavy!'

'Jellyfish!' I yelled in response, clinging to a rope. I was beginning to get the hang of this.

Peg-nose, however, was right. Despite the warm currents that had lifted us from our moorings back at Leisure Island, we were now over the cold sea and the cold air. Pigswill and cuttlefish, I thought, holding tightly to the edge of the basket. We *are* going down.

Ho and Molly soon realized and turned to me for help.

'Fret not, my nautical chums. I have the perfect plan!'

I turned away and gazed towards the horizon. What the blithering blue briny could I do now?

The waves lapped below us like beckoning fingers. I gulped a little.

There was no doubt about it – we were dropping closer and closer to the cold, cold ocean. There were no life jackets aboard and I wasn't sure whether my crew could swim. Not that it would do us any good – we were too far from the beach to survive a swim.

Peg-nose Pedro, the cursed villain, was giggling and rotating his nose even more. Then, worse still, he dropped his breeches, turned his back and taunted us with his bare bottom. Was there no end to this man's villainy? Wiggling his rear end in that unsavoury manner! 'Twas then I noticed something interesting about his bottom. I squinted and, sure enough, there on his skinny rump was a tattoo. A tattoo of a curly anchor! The same tattoo we had found on the photocopy in the museum. Ha! There was our final proof of his guilt. I must remember to report his bottom to the police.

The sea was growing closer and the swirling waves tickled the underside of our basket. Slowly, very slowly, my feet started to get wet.

What a way to go! I thought. I wanted a heroic ending with cut-throat antics and a swashbuckling finale. But 'twas not to be. Sam Hawkins – just a plop in the ocean.

Suddenly a swordfish popped its inquisitive head out of the water and spied us. Ho and Molly were baling away wildly and failed to see the fish. It winked at me. I was sure it winked at me.

Spot was still flapping away, trying to drag us from a watery grave, but 'twas a wasted task. The balloon was huge and he was tiny in comparison.

Suddenly something whooshed through the air and landed with a splat in the basket. I looked down to see the swordfish frolicking in the shallow water of the basket. It winked at me again.

I tore my eyes from this odd sight and looked at my loyal crew. They steamed away at their fruitless task like the good and proper pirates they were. How could I manage without them?

Then a sad thought struck me – they might be good pirates, but I could do without their weight.

'Crew – we need to lose some weight!'

Molly looked down at her tummy.

'The lighter we are, the higher we can rise. 'Tis as simple as that!'

Molly looked about and then did a most noble thing – a gesture I will remember to my dying day. She kissed both Ho and myself on the forehead and then leaped overboard.

Ho and I rushed to the edge of the basket and stared into the splashing, crashing ocean. We could see our dearest Moll no more. She had been swallowed up by the ever hungry waves and was gone. Both Ho and I stifled a tear and set about baling once more.

The balloon rose slightly and we cleared the water. We were gaining distance on Peg-nose's balloon. The loathsome thief was peering at us intently. He'd stopped rotating his nose, I noticed.

Within minutes the two balloons were neck and neck, but Peg-nose still had the height advantage. We were level with the balloon in distance, but far below it in height. Suddenly I heard a gunshot. Scallops! Pegnose still had his pistol! I looked out of the balloon – Peg-nose was aiming at us. He pulled the trigger. I braced myself, but nothing happened. I looked again to see a seething Peg-nose clicking the trigger again and again.

'He's run out of ammunition!' I hooted, and gave Ho a high five.

'Twas at this point a fork fell into the basket. It landed next to the winking swordfish. Where had that come from? I strained my neck to look out of the basket and up towards Peg-nose's balloon. The Spanish fiend was dropping cutlery on us.

'He's trying to burst our balloon!' I announced as a spoon bounced off my head. He must have stolen the cutlery from the Drunken Sailor. What a devious mind.

Spot tugged madly at the rope and managed to shift us from beneath Peg-nose's balloon. Peg-nose himself came into view. He was brandishing a ladle. He hurled it at us. It bounced off the balloon and dropped towards the sea.

I heard him swear in Spanish. Then he produced a carving knife. I watched helplessly as he took aim with his beady little eye and released the knife. It spun through the air and hit the balloon. I waited to hear a hiss, but none came. The handle must have hit the balloon instead of the blade. Phew!

'Twas at this point I noticed we were starting to dip again. And quite fast this time.

Peg-nose ceased his cutlery hurling for a short moment to giggle and point. He even waved the Cutglass Cutlass to taunt us further.

'You're still too heavy!' he sneered.

Ho grabbed his hat and started to bale, but realized we hadn't yet touched the water. He fingered his hat nervously and looked about him. He was the only crew member left. He gulped.

For a short moment we looked at each other. And then he saluted, hugged me and jumped overboard. I heard a splosh, but couldn't bring myself to see my old pal go under.

Sadly, I waved at Spot to tug harder and we started to rise.

Within seconds I was level with Peg-nose. Only a few feet separated me from the cutlass, and it was a distance I was determined to close.

As I came level with Peg-nose he gazed at me in astonishment. I rose slowly and met him face to face.

'Heave-ho, my hearty!' I said.'Hand over the cutlass!'

'Don't be doh dupid!' he cried, waving it in the air. 'Id's mine and mine forever! On guard!'

He thrust the cutlass in my direction, striking a duelling pose.

I was a little confuddled by this, but kept my wits about me.

'You wouldn't fight an unarmed man, would you?' I asked.

Peg-nose thought about his answer.

'Yes,' he said with a shrug. 'On guard, Dam Hawkins!'

Whatever was I to do? I had nothing to fight this dastardly deed doer with, but fight I must. 'Tis a matter of honour amongst pirates.

I looked around the basket for something – anything – with which to fight Peg-nose. Then my eyes fell on the answer.

'On guard!' I replied, proudly grasping the swordfish. Its long snout protruded towards the amazed Pegnose. It winked at him.

'I can't fight a fish!' he snarled.

'On guard!' I said insistently.

Peg-nose shrugged and landed a strong blow to the fish, who giggled and straightened himself ready for a further fight.

And then we really set to it. I stabbed and parried like in days gone by. Peg-nose responded with the cuts and jabs of a well-versed pirate. The slap of fish on cutlass sounded across the ocean, and with mighty yells and bellows we fought away.

Peg-nose deftly side-stepped one of my thrusts, whirled around and stabbed back. I, too, sidestepped and the cutlass embedded itself in my balloon.

'I'm dorry!' said Peg-nose. 'I was aiming for your heart. I do apologize!'

I bowed. 'It matters not, back to the duel . . . On guard . . . !'

It was then that I heard the hissing sound and realized the balloon was going down for a third time.

Spot realized too and let go of the guide-rope. He gave me a farewell gesture and flew away. A parrot deserting a sinking balloon!

But I had little time for cowardly birds – Peg-nose's balloon was getting away, once more. I had no choice. I clambered on to the edge of the basket, placed the swordfish under my arm and leaped.

The split second I spent in the air seemed like an eternity. I glanced at the slavering lips of the waves below and then, with a clunk, landed in Peg-nose's basket.

Before I could get my breath, Peg-nose was upon me with the Cut-glass Cutlass. I struggled to keep it from my throat. He pushed me to the edge of the wildly swaying basket.

We both turned to see the rapidly deflating balloon plummet towards the sea below, where it was set upon by a gaggle of seagulls.

Peg-nose suddenly grabbed my nose and pulled.

'Get off my balloon!' he yelled in my ear.

Suddenly we both stopped. Our well-trained piratical senses were telling us something was wrong. Something was amiss. Something was a-changing. We both sniffed the air and listened. The wind was changing direction.

'We're heading back to land!' we said together, and started to fight again. The basket was very small, but we did our best. Minutes flew by as we swiped and sliced the air. A cut here, a thrust there.

But it was Peg-nose who was the dirtier fighter. In mid-parry he stopped and pointed at something behind me.

'Penguin!' he yelled. I spun to see. He kicked me in the shin and I squealed like a dolphin. I dropped down to rub my shin and, as I did so, Peg-nose snatched the swordfish from my grasp and hurled it overboard. It giggled as it fell.

Now Peg-nose had the upper hand.

He stood over me like a whaler about to harpoon his quarry.

'I could, of course, make fun of you, Dam Hawkins. I could taunt you and belittle you. Dat would be fun. However, I have a far better plan.' He looked out of the balloon. 'Land ho!' he yelled.

'What are you going to do with me?' I said, in a quaking voice.

He drew his lemon face close to mine.

'I'm going to 'lice off your dose!'

A sinister leer slithered across his face and he lifted the Cut-glass Cutlass high above his head.

And then the hissing began.

Peg-nose looked left.

Then he looked right.

I, however, being a clever pirate, looked *up*.

'You've burst your balloon!' I yelled merrily.

The raised cutlass had made a slit in the balloon which suddenly tore itself wide into a gash and then into a tear. The hissing became a bellow.

I laughed and pointed at the befuddled pirate. Then a thought struck me.

'If there's no air in the balloon . . . Argggghhhh!!!'

We both yelled wildly as we plummeted towards the earth.

☠   ☠

Thank Neptune for Whackett's Circus! It was directly below the balloon. We hit the canvas at a rapid speed and the tent collapsed around us.

When I awoke I heard muffled protests. I rolled over and saw the octopus smothering Peg-nose Pedro. At first I thought they were dancing some sort of aquatic rumba. But I soon realized the octopus had snared Peg-nose in its strong tentacles and was awaiting the police. 'Twas clear he'd loathed his time working for Mr X and now was the moment he'd been longing for.

Soon, Stibbins and Stump came scrambling through the mass of canvas, puffing and panting. They grabbed Peg-nose.

Pulling the battered photocopy from my pocket, I called out weakly, 'Investigate his bottom!'

Stibbins pulled down Peg-nose's breeches. She and Stump compared his bottom to the photocopy and, convinced they were the same, handcuffed him and led him away.

I rolled back over to discover the Cut-glass Cutlass safely by my side.

I batted my way through the canvas and finally felt the sunlight on my face.

A small crowd had gathered on the edge of the circus, including Whackett, the Mayor and a few midgets, who had been watching amazed at the events above them. They applauded long and loud as I slowly but triumphantly walked towards them, holding aloft the legendary Cut-glass Cutlass. And behind me scuttled the octopus, its sad expression replaced by something not unlike a smile.

CHAPTER NINETEEN

The pilchards stared at me from the tin. I poked at them with my fork, but I wasn't hungry. I'd not eaten much since the end of the case two days ago. I prodded them some more and tried to regain my appetite, but 'twas no use.

The old Naughty Lass was as silent as the deep.

Spot squatted on my shoulder. Neither a squawk nor a chirrup had passed his beak in two days. After deserting my sinking balloon he'd come straight back home and hidden under the settee. It took me a while to convince him I wasn't angry. We were friends again now.

I gazed out of the porthole of my bedroom, over the fields and towards the distant horizon. The sun was slowly rising and I had not slept a wink all night. In the distance a lone seagull swooped.

I sighed and offered the tin of pilchards to Spot. He shook his head and looked away. I don't think parrots can cry, but if he could he would have done. I produced a hanky and dabbed his eyes anyway, then I blew a resounding blast with my nose.

I placed the pilchards to one side and sat quietly.

All was silent save for the ticking of the bedroom clock.

I had sat in my squeaky, creaky rocking chair all night, turning the events over in my mind. I kept reliving my last moments with Ho and Molly again and again. How could I have let them do it? What a noble pair! I should have taken their place! How would I ever find their like again? Crew members so devoted they would surrender their lives for their captain. The Cut-glass Cutlass had been rescued and our mystery was solved, but the triumphant finale I had hoped for had turned to ashes.

I looked at the pilchards once more. I wondered what young Ho would have made with them. They suddenly seemed a lot more tasty when I thought of Ho's cooking, and I nibbled at one for a moment.

☠   ☠

A slight drizzle filled the air as I trudged towards the town museum. I didn't feel like being a guest of honour, but the Mayor had insisted. I eeled my way into my best frock coat, greased down my hair and placed a sprig of seaweed in my lapel. I even made a little bow tie for Spot.

At the museum a huge crowd had gathered. 'Twasn't all for old Sam, you understand. Today was the grand unveiling of the Cut-glass Cutlass, though they were going to give me some award or other.

On the podium the Mayor waffled through her speech, but my thoughts were drifting elsewhere. She muttered about my bravery and suchlike and how grateful the town was to have the cutlass back. She also mentioned Molly and Ho, which was kind.

Suddenly, I heard my name. I woke myself from my thoughts and looked up. The crowd was applauding and the Mayor was beckoning me to the lectern. I slowly walked over.

'And as a memento of this great occasion,' she said, 'the town of Washed-upon-the-Beach would like to give Sam Hawkins its highest award – the Golden Albatross.'

She produced the Golden Albatross, a small medal on a ribbon, and hung it round my neck. I peered at it, a little bemused. I muttered some words of thanks and went back to my seat.

'And now the moment we have all been waiting for,' said the Mayor. 'Without further ado, I am proud to unveil the Cut-glass Cutlass.'

She tugged a small rope and a velvety curtain swished back to reveal the cutlass. 'Twas a beautiful and stirring sight, I must admit, but I couldn't help thinking what I'd lost to acquire it.

Later, on the museum steps, a gaggle of photographers swarmed about me. Journalists were shouting questions and jabbing those micronophone things under my nose.

'Tell us how you got hold of the cutlass, Sam!' shouted one.

I braced myself and launched into the tale, but the words felt dry in my mouth. "Twas a staggering tale of derring-do, me hearties. I've swashed buckles on the highest of seas, but never have I had an adventure to match this. 'Twas a tale of intrigue and mystery, of danger and terror, of skulduggery and . . .'

Suddenly a mobile phone chirruped and a spotty journalist answered it.

'Hello?'

The others hushed him and urged me to continue my tale.

'. . . of skulduggery and danger and terror . . .'

'Yes, you already mentioned the danger and terror,' another sighed.

'A tale of derring-do and near disaster then,' I offered.

The spotty journalist suddenly shouted, 'You're not going to believe this!'

All the others turned like a shoal of fish in his direction.

'The round-the-world water-skiing record has just been broken by "Yank" Swiftly. He's arriving on the beach right now!'

And with that he slipped the phone in his pocket and ran off in the direction of the beach. After a few mutterings all the other journalists followed. Within minutes I was left alone on the steps with a parrot on my shoulder and a Golden Albatross around my neck.

I sniffed, looked up at the clouds and sighed.

Hey-ho, I thought, such is fame.

☠   ☠

Later that night, as I sat in the still hold of the Naughty Lass, writing up my case notes by spluttering candlelight, a knock came at the door.

When I answered it I could see nothing but a huge box.

'Could you sign for this?' said a voice.

I peered around the box to see a sweating delivery man.

'What is it?' I asked.

'Dunno.' He shrugged. 'Looks like a box of mobile phones.'

'I didn't order any mobile phones,' I said, as dark thoughts trickled into my brain.

'You are Sam Hawkins?' he asked.

'Yes.'

'And this is the Naughty Lass?'

'Yes.'

'You'd better sign here, then!'

He thrust his clipboard at me and I scribbled on it. He soon departed.

I dragged the box into the centre of the living room. Was this Peg-nose Pedro's revenge? Had he sent me some diabolical gift? Would it explode?

I walked around the box a couple of times. I thought for a moment and decided to ignore it. I wasn't going to open it. I'd take it away tomorrow and dump it somewhere.

I sat down at my desk and started to scribble my notes once more.

'Twas at this point I heard something that at first intrigued and then delighted me.

'Twas singing.

I looked about and listened.

'Twas an old sea-shanty.

I looked about me again. A smile came to my salty lips and I tossed my quill aside.

I ran over to the box. Spot flapped over and landed on top.

The singing was coming from within.

And singing the shanty were two voices. Two voices I recognized.

I tore open the lid of the box with my trusty blade and dug into the polystyrene pieces inside. I rummaged around and my hand felt the top of a hat –

'Ho!' I screamed.

My other hand felt a large, slightly balding head.

'Molly!' I cried.

And with that my old crew mates burst from the box in a shower of polystyrene like two performing dolphins.

I hugged them both heartily.

'But how? Where? When?' I spluttered.

'It's simple, Sam,' explained Ho. 'When we fell from the balloon we bobbed about a bit and then got rescued by a boat.'

'And it was a boat carrying a consignment of mobile phones to Peg-nose Pedro!' continued Molly.

'We just changed the address on the box, climbed in and waited!'

'And that's how we ended up back here!'

Molly and Ho climbed from the box and we hugged like long-lost cousins. I suddenly snatched up my squeeze-box and began to pump out a shanty. Molly grabbed Ho by the hand and Spot by the wing and led them in a merry dance around the settee. What a glorious sight to see my old swabbies back on board. What adventures we had to look forward to! The music swirled through the air and Ho, Molly, Spot and I jigged the night away. We toasted each other with tea and sang many a happy shanty of life on the ocean waves.

Eventually we collapsed in a giggling heap and Ho went to make some cocoa.

I gazed up at the painting of my mum. She seemed to be smiling at me.

'I got it back for you!' I said happily. 'And it won't be the last mystery solved by Sam Hawkins, Pirate Detective!'

Sam Hawkins is no one-ship wonder!
Look out for him in Ian Billings'
second swashbuckling story of

Sam Hawkins: Pirate Detective
And The Pointy Head Lighthouse

Sam Hawkins, Pirate Detective,
nets some very fishy goings on when
the Pointy Head Lighthouse is kidnapped
in the broadest of broad daylight.

But Sam never misses a trip
and soon takes on this tanglesome teaser,
but a distinct lack of clues has run him aground . . .
until a ransom note from the Scarlet Winkle arrives.

Will Sam winkle out the Winkle?
Can he save the lighthouse,
his job, and the day?